LAVRON

LAVRON

Stephen J Breen

Tellwell Talent
www.tellwell.ca

ISBN
978-0-2288-6006-8 (Hardcover)
978-0-2288-6005-1 (Paperback)
978-0-2288-6007-5 (eBook)

This story would not have been possible without
the guidance of my editor/ sister
Cheryle Da Ponte and the support of my loving wife Traci

Introduction to Lavron

Missouri is one of the most diverse States in America. Beautiful landscapes mixed with rugged terrain, tremendous waterways, forests and even mountains contribute to this divergent landmass. The State capital, Jefferson City is on the Missouri river and is one of the cleanest cities in the country.

Eighty miles southwest of Jefferson City off of highway # 54 is the small town of Lavron. A quaint tourist town, Lavron boasts one of the best places to fish, hunt, hike and even bird watch. The scenery is captivating. Any picture that is taken here could be used as a post card. Many vacationers believe that Lavron and the surrounding area is the best kept secret, and return annually.

Like most small towns, the residents of Lavron are set in their ways. They are used to the spike in population in the Spring and Summer months and take it with a grain of salt. They realize that tourists provide revenue for their town and are friendly, for the most part. Lavron is fairly large in area, but has had just six thousand residents for the last dozen years. It seems that everybody knows everyone and that's how a tight community works.

When the news broke about a major car parts company wanting to build a massive plant in Lavron, the citizens became quite concerned. Grayson Manufacturing International is a significant player in car and truck parts, and building a plant in Lavron would be perfect for distribution throughout the States, and would take some of the manufacturing burden from the other Grayson plants. It would be a paramount endeavor and one that Grayson Manufacturing wants done. Surely, Lavron's Town Council would not approve such an undertaking. It would certainly disrupt the town and Lavron is just fine the way it is. The consensus is that the good citizens of Lavron want nothing to do with Grayson Manufacturing invading their village and if push comes to shove, the citizens are prepared to shove!

LAVRON

Chapter 1

As the middle of March approached, the weather in Lavron is warming up. The snow has dissipated and no ice remains on the rivers or lakes. To the residents of Lavron, this is the best time of year. It seemed that the town woke up after what is usually a dramatic winter. Business owners are opening their stores and putting their wares out as people casually walk and shop. In about a month the angler's will start flowing in. The coffee shops are crammed with residents gossiping and predicting what this year's biggest catch will be. There is excitement in the air mixed with a little anxiety.

Buzz Wheeler looked forward to the influx of fishermen and hikers this time of year. Owning the town's only fishing and hunting establishment, he had his hands full keeping up with the inventory. As he pulled into his regular parking spot behind the store, Buzz wonders what supplies will show up today. He grabbed his bagged lunch from the seat beside him and crawls out of his 1996 Ford pickup.

Walking the twelve feet to the back door Buzz felt the warmth of the sun on his neck and thinks, it won't be long now. He twists the key and the solid oak door opened with a creak. It is just before eight am.

Lavron Lure's was established by Buzz's parents in the early seventies. Yvonne and Dave Wheeler bought the older building from a retiring taxidermist. Within a month they were open business was booming. As Buzz does today, Yvonne and Dave sold everything from hooks to canoes. Narrow aisles and creaky hardwood floors gives character to the store, not to mention the stuffed animals hanging from the rafters that were left behind.

The first thing Buzz does each morning after opening up is get a pot of coffee brewing. The aroma is enticing. More than a few customers have asked if they could buy a cup. With a smile on his face, Buzz asks, cream and sugar?

Fishing season opens in early April and anglers from all parts of the country come to Lavron Lure's to stock up, not only for the great prices but the great service Buzz and his team provide. "If we don't have it, we will find it." That's Buzz's motto.

There are too many rivers, streams and offshoots to mention in and around Lavron, but Lake of the Ozark's is only half a mile down the road. Lake of the Ozark's was created in 1931 after Union Light and Power dammed the Osage river. With its eight generators the Bagnell dam as it was named, supplies hydroelectric power to St. Louis and the surrounding region. It also created a massive sixty-one thousand square mile lake with eleven hundred miles of shoreline. Today it is home to over two hundred species of fish.

Jim Lambert, a long time friend of Buzz's pushed through the big red door of Lavron Lure's, ringing the bell at the top. "Good morning Buzz. Boy the coffee is smelling terrific," Jim yells to the back of the store. "You are just in time Jimmy. The usual?" Buzz says while reaching for two mugs.

Both Buzz and Jim are lifelong friends, and residents of Lavron. Buzz being a year older than Jim at 58 is tall and slim with almost all of his hair. Jim on the other hand is five foot eight, a little over weight and is losing his hair. His wire rimmed glasses make him look quite distinguished. Jim is the Editor of the local newspaper, The Lavron Herald. The once a week rag comes out on Thursday's with all the news a small town can muster. Throughout the winter months, news can be hard to find. Jim is looking forward to the upcoming season just to fill more pages. As the two friends sipped on their coffee, the conversation goes right to the fishing derby that Buzz sponsors annually. "It seems more people participate in your derby each year Buzz. This year should be no different," Jim says matter of factly. "It sure seems that way Jim. By the way, I'll take a quarter page advertisement in the Herald this year and run it for the next three weeks. I want to make sure no one misses out."

Lavron Lure's offers lucrative prizes for the three-day derby. For a ten-dollar entry fee and some good luck, you could win rods, reels, tackle and the grand prize for the largest fish, a canoe! This is a tax write off for Buzz and at the same time, brings in a lot of business. The fishing derby itself is held the first week of April right when the season opens. "I have my eye on that canoe," Jim says with a grin pointing to the canoe hanging above the counter. "If I had a nickel for every time I heard that Jim, I would have a dollar," Buzz chuckles. "Well Buzz my friend, I have a new spot picked out on the lake, that I think will be very productive. By the way, I best get my license while I'm here," Jim digs into his pocket for his wallet.

"There is another reason I dropped in this morning Buzz," Jim getting serious now. "What's on your mind bud?" Buzz looking up from the counter. "I don't know how true this is but, rumor has it that Grayson Manufacturing is looking at a large piece of land over on Draper street. They figure Lavron is an ideal place to ship their goods from. We are centrally located to distribute car parts across the States apparently," Jim shrugs his shoulders. "That is ridiculous Jim! Grayson has been charged more than once for polluting rivers. Once in Philadelphia for polluting the Delaware river and I believe another one in Portland," Buzz be animated waving his arms. Jim jumps in. "Yes, they were charged, but if you look back, both times their high priced lawyers got them off with a slap on the wrist. Now, as I was told, they want to build a state-of-the-art manufacturing site right here in the industrial part of town," Jim's blood pressure rising. "Well let's just see what develops from this rumor. I can't see the Town Council approving such a project," Buzz shakes his head and starts putting fishing line on the shelves. "Let's hope you are right Buzz. Lavron certainly doesn't need a polluting manufacturing plant," Jim turns to leave. "Don't you worry Jim. Lavron will always be our quaint hospitable town."

Chapter 2

As the Spring days' fly by, Lavron grows. Many anglers, hikers and bird watcher flock to the small town. With over 435 different species of birds, it is the best place to find such beauty. One of the prettiest birds in the region is the Missouri State bird, the Blue bird, but Snow Owls, Woodpeckers, Warblers, Sandpipers and Cranes are plentiful as well. Hunters also come to see the birds, but that isn't until autumn. And all they want to see is the ducks, geese and wild turkeys, for obvious reasons.

Lavron has three Motels and they are usually vacant throughout the winter. It is no wonder the owner's welcome springtime and the influx of vacationers. Busy cleaning the rooms, snack bars and parking lots for the upcoming season they were counting on the revenue. Other than the motels, there are eight campgrounds in the surrounding area and they fill up quickly. Without a reservation, accommodations can be futile this time of year.

The residents of Lavron take the vacationers/ anglers with a grain of salt. They realize that the town thrives on the incoming traffic, but at the same time, they love their peace and quiet. The population of Lavron is and has been six thousand for the last dozen years. People visit here, but they don't move here unless they retire. It's like a sleepy little town right out of one of Aesop's fables, in the winter months anyway.

Troy and Traci Laurie own one of the motels. The Ozark Inn has been in Troy's family for generations. Passed down from grandparents to parents to Troy and his wife. Troy's parents still reside in an end unit of the Inn and try to help as much as possible. Troy being an avid fisherman himself, loves to get out onto the lake and fish the day away. That doesn't happen as often anymore as the reservations increace and the motel slowly fills. With two stories and twenty-six units to look after, it keeps them hopping.

Lavron has the essentials but not much else. With only two groceries and three variety stores, picking your time to shop is key. Most of the town's people wait till Monday or Tuesday to do their groceries as more and more vacationers invade the area. There are three restaurants to choose from if you didn't want to buy groceries. There is the Bluebird Bistro, featuring a smaller but elegant atmosphere, and we have Hungry Hank's, that is popular with families as they offer, Catch of the Day. This is usually either Walleye or Bass. They also offer, All You Can Eat, but only on weekdays.

And then of course there is a McDonald's.

Lavron also has two taverns if you are looking for a cold beverage and Roadhouse food. The Elk's Hangout is a sportsman's bar with hunting trophies and fishing nets hanging on the barn board walls. It's a good place to drink and tell lies. The other bar is The River Piper. It is the more popular of the two. The younger generation seem to congregate there for the loud music and dance floor.

The three coffee shops in Lavron are a Godsend for the early riser. Strong coffee, donuts, eggs and even pancakes can be eaten in, or taken out. For a fee they will even provide a bagged lunch. Dunkin Donuts is the only franchise, the other two are privately owned. All three are usually very busy as a they are key meeting spots both in store and in the parking lot.

The one other place deemed essential would be the Lavron Library. For a town the size of Lavron, it's Library is huge. Dating back to 1934 the town has added two additions to its place of literature and learning.

The town's Librarian, Laura Rush has worked there since college, some thirty years. She runs the place like it's her own. Meticulously neat and tidy, she is like a drill Sargent if you raise your voice.

The two things Lavron does not have, are a Community Centre and a Movie Theatre. Last election Mayor Steven Taylor promised to build both with the revenue from the last term. That was enough to vote Mayor Taylor in for a second session. His promises seem to have faded after the election, and the residents of Lavron have not forgotten that. The Mayor has been treading water very carefully ever since.

Chapter 3

April has now arrived in Lavron. The thermometer is breaking the seventy-degree mark and the sun is shining bright. Laura Rush climbs the steps of the Library and reaches inside her purse for the keys. It is almost 9 am and Laura is surprised to see three gentlemen in suits standing at the door. "Good morning men." Laura said glancing at her watch. "Good morning ma'am," One of the men replied. Laura recognized one of the guy's as the town's civil engineer, George Hansen. "What brings you here so early George?" Laura asked pryingly. "As you can see, I have some guests from out of town. I was wondering if you could dig up some old surveys for them? They are interested in a parcel of land on Draper street." George mentioned not quite whispering. "Well, let's see what we can find." Laura said while turning the key to the old grey building. Laura clicked on the lights and went to the back of the Library where all the old records are kept.

The three gentlemen find a large oak table, take off their suit jackets and opened their briefcases. As Laura returned with the rolled up surveys, she can't help but see a letterhead with Grayson Manufacturing International printed on it. She does her best to conceal the shock she felt. "I hope you gentlemen find these surveys adequate. They haven't seen the light of day in decades." Laura places the surveys on the table. "Thank you Ma'am," said one of the strangers. Mike Hayes is tall, fit and very intelligent. Being the CEO of Grayson Manufacturing he is well placed. His colleague Bill Landry, the CFO, is just as well qualified being a graduate from MIT.

As the three men study the surveys Laura ensures that she stays close by. Just around the corner and behind a book case, she can still hear what was being said. Studying the drawings, Mike Hansen points at the survey and explains, "This land is what Grayson is looking for George. The price is reasonable, and I'm sure we can negotiate a lower tax bracket if Grayson were to purchase this piece of land?" "I'm sure we can make some kind of arrangement Mike." George says with a smile. Mike looks at the CFO, Bill Landry and says, "These dozen acres would be centrally located for the distribution of our products throughout the States. What do you think Bill?" Bill being the shorter of the two executives with a little extra weight around the midsection, analyzed the drawings carefully and said; "Clearing the land and building a five hundred thousand square foot facility would take approximately two years. And that's providing we can have access in and out of town around the clock." Bill says questionably to both Mike and George. "I will sit down with the town council and work out any details that need to be taken care of guy's," explains George with sincerity. "That sounds good George. Here is my card. Give me a shout next week after you have discussed our intentions." Mike glances at the drawings once again then rolls them up, saying, "Let's hope Grayson Manufacturing International and the town of Lavron can work out a deal. I feel that it would be good for both parties." George elaborates, "I will be in touch with you gents within a week, one way or another." The men shake hands, closed their briefcases and headed for the exit.

Laura Rush could not believe what she overheard. There is no way the town council would pass a bill of this magnitude. Especially with Grayson's reputation. She dug the cell out of her purse and called Jim Lambert.

Chapter 4

The phone rings eight times and with every ring Laura becomes more frantic. Finally, "Good morning, Lavron Herald." Jim Lambert says. "Jim, It's Laura Rush at the Library." "What can I do for you Laura?" Jim questioned. "I think it's best if we meet privately Jim. I have some disturbing news that could affect all of Lavron." Jim knows Laura. She is a sweet lady but likes to exaggerate. "Ok Laura, I am busy now, but if this news is that important, would you care to have a drink after work and discuss it?" Queried Jim. "That would be fine. I get off work at five. Can we meet at the River Piper?' Laura asked. "Five o'clock it is Laura. See you then." Jim hung the phone up wondering what disturbing news Laura could possibly have.

Jim walked into the River Piper at 4:50 pm. It is dark and it takes him a minute to focus. The Piper is large with a dance floor, stage and huge speakers mounted on the wall, not to mention a twenty-foot solid oak bar that they keep polished. Jim sees Laura already sitting in a booth away from everyone. Jim greets Laura with a smile and hand shake. "So what is this disturbing news Laura?" Jim asks with sincerity as he sits across from her.

The two order a couple of beers. When their beverages arrive, Laura stares at Jim and states; "Jim, I am beside myself. George Hansen came into the Library today with two strangers from out of town. These men are from Grayson Manufacturing. They are looking to purchase twelve acres of land on Draper Street. They want to build a five hundred square foot plant." Laura trying to keep her voice down but being animated at the same time. "I heard a rumor a month ago about Grayson's interest in Lavron. But it faded fast. Now, are you sure Laura? How did you get this information? Jim being skeptical. "I got it right from the horse's mouth. I overheard the conversation." Laura remarks. "I hardly think that Lavron would even consider such an endeavor. We have all heard about Grayson's law suits." Jim shaking his head. "Apparently George will bring it up with the town council in the next meeting on Thursday." Laura states. "Well, I think that we should get as many people as possible to that meeting. That way the council will see that the residents of Lavron won't put up with this ridiculous venture." Jim's blood pressure is beginning to show.

As the two sit talking about how to go about getting the town together, in regards to Grayson's inquest, Greg and Brock Duchin walk through the door of the Piper. The twin Brothers are the town's football heroes. Playing for SLU for four years, the boys are well recognized around town. They are big men. Line Backers. The twins are not identical but have similar traits. Both are blonde and weigh well over two hundred fifty pounds.

They are very friendly but, do not piss them off! They work full time for the Works Department in town, and work part time at the River Piper as door men.

Jim sees the pair as they come through the door. He knows then how the word about Grayson could get around quickly. Jim knew the guy's, as he covered many of the games they played. St. Louis University produces many NFL players, but as Line Backers, the Duchin brothers were about twenty-five pounds' shy of what an NFL averaged. Jim waves the brothers over to the table. "Hello boy's. How are you doing?" Jim says with a grin. "Not bad at all Jim. Good to see you." Greg reaching to shake Jim's hand. "Greg and Brock, this is Laura Rush. She is the town Librarian, not that you two have seen a Library." Jim laughing. "Funny Jim, and pleased to meet you Laura." Greg and Brock leaning over to shake Laura's hand. "My pleasure guy's." Laura says blushing. Jim lowering his voice so that the brothers have to lean in, explained; "Boy's it seems we have an urgent issue that needs to be taken care of. We have gotten wind, that a huge car parts company wants to build a mammoth plant over on Draper Street. Lavron is not the place for a project of that size." Jim is sweating as he is talking and then takes a swig of his beer. "We have enough trouble with the population of Lavron every year starting now. With the vacationers, anglers etc., we are at capacity. If a company like Grayson Manufacturing moves in, where is everyone supposed to live?" Jim lowering his head almost lost. "I have heard of Grayson." Brock interjects. "When we were in Philadelphia playing ball, there was a big law suit against them for polluting the Delaware. I believe they got off." "Yes they did" Laura blurts. "And also in Portland Oregon for polluting the Columbia river. Lavron does not want or need Grayson Manufacturing.

"What can we do to help?" Greg asks. Jim jumps in. "We need to get the word out that Lavron may consider Grayson's request. The subject will be brought up on Thursday at the council meeting. You boys know a lot of people in town. Will you let everyone you know that we need as many residents from town at that meeting?" Both Greg and Brock look at each other and nod. "You bet Jim. Give us a couple days. We'll have a crowd show up." "That is terrific Guy's." Jim and Laura feeling relieved.

"I hate to change the subject Jim." Brock states. "But this won't affect Buzz Wheeler's fishing derby, will it? The town is filling up with all the fishermen and families." Jim glances up at the brothers and declared; "I don't think this would affect Buzz's derby. Although many people from town participate in it. The council meeting is Thursday. The derby starts Friday." Laura speaks up: "Well it will sure give the citizens of Lavron something to talk about." Jim finishes his beer and says; "I better get over to Lavron Lure's and let Buzz know what's happening. I know I can count on you guy's to spread the word. And Laura, thanks for the news." With that Jim slowly gets up from the booth. "You can be sure the word will be heard Jim." Brock announced.

As Jim pulls into the parking lot of Lavron Lure's, he is surprised to see that there are no parking spaces. He pulls his white Audi back onto the street and puts it in park. The store is busy. The aisles are narrow and it seems the store is at capacity. Buzz is standing by the cash register at the back of the store. Jim eases through the crowd and approaches Buzz. "Hi Buzz. I can see that you are quite busy. Everyone is pumped for your derby on Friday." Jim assures Buzz. "Busy isn't the word Jim. Swamped is more like it. This year may be a record for the most participance. And it's a good thing that I hired a couple of students." Buzz said punching in some purchases into the cash register. "Do you remember me telling you about a rumor I heard about Grayson Manufacturing looking at some land here in town?" Jim exclaimed. "Ya, I remember Jim. What have you heard now?" Buzz inquiring. "Exactly that Buzz! Laura Rush overheard a conversation at the Library with George Hansen and a couple of executives from Grayson. They are interested in twelve acres of land on Draper Street and want to build a five hundred thousand square foot manufacturing plant. He is bringing the subject up at the council meeting on Thursday. We need to get everyone we know at that meeting." Jim declared. "I totally agree Jimmy. I'll be there right after I close for the evening. Buzz expresses. "Awesome Buzz. By the way, we have the Duchin boy's spreading the word as well.

I have a feeling that we will be well represented at the council meeting." Jim reassures. "I wonder what George Hansen was thinking. He knows how busy and crammed Lavron gets in the spring and summer months." Buzz shaking his head. "Well, we will set the town council straight Buzz. And I will see you there." Jim says as he turned to leave.

Chapter 5

Three days' pass. The word about Grayson gets around Lavron quickly. The town was buzzing, and not in a good way. Usually everyone was gearing up for the annual fishing derby but, it seems the residents of Lavron have a bigger challenge this year. The subject was on every bodies minds and the talk was, let's squash any chance Grayson has of obtaining that land. Everyone is to be at the Town Council meeting ten minutes early to show their support.

Jim Lambert, Laura Rush and Greg and Brock Duchin arrive a little earlier than they expect. They, along with Buzz Wheeler wanted front row seats to this fiasco. They watch as Buzz pulls into the parking lot, then wave him over to be first into the chamber. Laura had done some homework on Grayson Manufacturing International and she was carrying a couple of binders. "I dug up some dirt on Grayson." Laura mentions to the guy's. "I have the court documents regarding their law suits in Philadelphia and Oregon. There is no way they should have gotten away with polluting the rivers." Laura was almost in tears. "Well today is another day Laura and the environmental laws have changed. They are much stricter." Buzz interjects.

The parking lot has never been as full as it is today. Not everyone that shows up will be able to get in. There will be standing room only and some will have to be turned away. As a security guard unlocks the doors to the council chamber, he cannot believe his eyes. *What the heck is going on here?* All he can do is open the doors and tell everyone to stay in single file. Twenty minutes later the council chamber was packed with concerned residents. The room explodes with anger as the council began taking their seats.

The Mayor himself couldn't believe the size of the crowd. Before he sat in his plush armed chair, Mayor Steven Taylor held his hand's high in the air and asked for quiet and order. "I know why you are all here and please let me tell you that Grayson International is the real deal." Mayor Taylor insisted. With that a burst of mayhem in ensued. A bottle came flying passed the Mayors head. Security was all around looking for trouble makers. The Mayor spoke once again. "Please calm down everyone. Let me try to explain." There is a bit of a hush. "Thank-you. Our Civil engineer George Hansen met with the CEO and CFO of Grayson Manufacturing. Lavron is key for Grayson's success. If they were to obtain the twelve acres of land in the Industrial part of town, namely Draper Street, they would build a State-of-the-art, five hundred thousand square foot manufacturing plant. The revenue from that project would help Lavron significantly." Mayor Taylor stating sincerely. Laura Rush stood. "And what do you have to say about Grayson's reputation for polluting waterways Mr. Mayor?" Laura yells waving the two binders. "I do believe the charges were dropped, were they not Ms. Rush?" Mayor Taylor remarked. At that point the room blew up! The crowd stood yelling and screaming. More objects being thrown towards the members of council. One of the security guards runs to the microphone and declares the meeting over. The members of council duck and run to safety. Mayor Taylor called the council to a huddle behind the scenes. "I believe George Hansen and myself should let Grayson know what our town thinks of their ambitions. Set up a meeting will you George?" Mayor Steven Taylor said, in defeat.

Friday morning comes almost like Christmas morning. Every angler was up early anticipating the biggest present. A record sized fish. Buzz was already at the store setting up the scale outside in the parking lot when the sun made its appearance. Not a cloud in the sky and the Weather man predicted a warm day. Greg and Brock Duchin were already at the Lake of the Ozark's sipping on coffee. "I can't believe how many people are out so soon. For a lake this size, it is pretty crowded." Greg said to Brock "It sure is. But, let's try our luck over by the weeds. Guaranteed the Walleye are hanging around in there." Brock points to a spot under a bunch of Dogwood trees. "Sounds good bro." The twin's grabbed their fishing gear and headed towards the shaded area where the Dogwoods and weeds are. The guy's saw many familiar faces, but even more unfamiliar as they passed through the trees and rocks heading to their spot.

There are many strategic fishing spots in and around Lake of the Ozark's. Some prefer fishing from the dam, others like Greg and Brock know the lake better than most and have their own little places to throw a line in the water. But it seems now that there are more boats on the lake than usual. If all these people fishing are in Buzz's derby, it will be a record amount of participants. Brock sees Troy Laurie from the Ozark Inn standing on the shore and casting a line into the water. "Good morning Troy. Thought you might be too busy at the Inn to come out today?" Brock says with a smile. "Hi boy's. Yes, we are quite busy but, I thought I could manage a few hours out here before everyone wakes up. I have caught a couple two and three-pound Bass but, I want the winner." Troy remarks reeling his line in. "Good luck with that Troy. We'll show you what the winner looks like." Greg jabbed as the guy's trekked by. "Ok ladies, if you want to see the trophy, drop by some time." Troy said laughing.

The Duchin brothers find their spot, set their fishing tackle down and hook up lures to the line.

After launching their Spinners into the water by the weeds, the twins sit on the rocks and relaxed. The sun was above the trees now and the temperature rising. A perfect day for fishing. Five minutes into it, Greg got a bite. "Holy smokes Brock. Just got a nice bite. This may be the spot." Greg says excitedly. And just then Brock got something on his line and it was putting up a fight. "Yup, here we go brother. I have a fighter." Brock exclaimed as he fought with his fish. It took a few minutes but Brock reels in a huge Catfish. "Wow, let's get that baby on the stringer. I bet it's six pounds." Greg announces patting Brock on the back. Brock grabs the stringer out of his tackle box and with a minor struggle got his Catfish hooked on.

The twin brothers only fish for two more hours when they reach their limit. Six fish each. To their dismay the Catfish was the biggest. But they have also caught seven Walleye, three Bass and two Catfish. "We have enough for a couple fish fries." Greg says eyeing their catch. "Yes we do bro, but let's see how the much the big Catfish weighs. It's got to be in the running." Brock declares. "OK. We'll go to Buzz's store to see exactly what she weighs. It might just get you a prize." Greg states. "With all these other anglers out here, someone's going to catch a fish bigger than mine." Brock adds. "That may be true Brock, but if so, we have two more days to fish." Greg says packing up their gear.

As the brother's hike out of their fishing spot they can't help but notice how many more people have come out to try their luck.

"This is crazy! Look at how many people are here now." Greg remarks being astounded. "We better let Buzz know that, he better put a limit on how many people he allows in the derby next year. This is ridiculous." Brock observes. "No wonder Lavron is stretched to capacity this time of year. And the council wants to grant Grayson their wish. Haha. They better change their minds or there's going to be trouble." Greg utters. "We'll see what transpires in the next week or two. Mayor Turner should realize that our town will not play host to a polluting manufacturing giant. It's just not in the cards. Lavron will not be pushed into this." Brock threatens.

The twins make it back to Greg's Dodge pick-up and loaded their tackle into the back. They can't wait to get to Lavron Lure's and let Buzz know what they observed. Not to mention weighing Brock's Catfish.

Twenty minutes later the guy's pull into the parking lot of Buzz's store. It is packed. There is a line up at the scale, everyone hoping for a contender and a prize. The winning fish so far is a Large Mouth Bass weighing 4 pounds 7 ounces. Greg and Brock looked at each other and can't wait for their turn at the scale. As they near the scale they see

Buzz talking to other clients. "Buzz!" Greg roars getting his attention. "Hey boy's. Looks like you may have a challenger there." Buzz declares pointing at the Catfish. "We are hoping so Buzz, but listen, Greg and I think that you should put a Cap on the amount of people you let participate in your Derby. The lake is crowded. We have never seen that many anglers out there at once." Brock announces. "Oh come on now guy's, I admit that I had a record amount of entrance's this year, but it is opening weekend for fishing and everyone is stoked to get out after a long winter. You know how busy Lavron gets in the spring and summer months. Buzz states. "Ya, we know Buzz, but if this is just the start of the season, we will be over capacity before you know it." Greg mentions. "And what would happen if Grayson got their way and moved in?" Brock uttered. "Don't you worry boy's, that will not happen. Now let's see what your fish weighs." Brock hooked his Catfish onto the scale and was shocked to see, 6 pounds, 4 ounces. "This is the largest Catfish so far guy's. Congratulations. I hope this holds up until Sunday afternoon when it's all done." Buzz says smiling. "Thanks Buzz. We'll be back on Sunday to collect the winning prize." Brock jousts. "You do that guy's. I'm going to try my luck on the river when I finally get out of here this evening. I'll see if there is a Sturgeon to be caught. Wouldn't that be funny if I won my own derby." Buzz says jokingly. "That would be funny Buzz. We didn't think to try the river. But there is always tomorrow. Good luck Buzz.

Talk to you soon." And with that, the twin brothers were gone.

The Derby went for two more days. Buzz never did get out fishing as people were coming at all times to get their catch weighed. There were a lot of stories about the big one that got away, but the thing that is on everyone's minds is Grayson Manufacturing International. The people of Lavron speculated that the town council were being bribed. Why else would they even consider such a huge endeavor? The residents of Lavron certainly made it clear that they are totally against Grayson's bid.

Buzz's Derby was a success. Brock did end up winning the largest Catfish and collected a new Diawa rod and reel. The largest Bass was

4.7 pounds and the largest Walleye was 5.6 pounds. Each of those contestants won prizes as well. No one won the canoe as there were no 10 pound and over fish this year. Jim Lambert was embarrassed that he had no contenders after telling Buzz about his plans. With the Derby being over now, everyone from town went back to their own lives, as the vacationers kept things hopping. The three Motels are at capacity as well as all eight campgrounds. The scenery around Lavron is second to none. Hikers, anglers and bird watchers gather here each year for the sheer beauty. And after a day on the trails or water, everyone likes a cold beverage and bite to eat at one of the town's taverns. The revenue is welcome and the residents are friendly to a point. A couple times in the past, tourists have had a few too many drinks and became rowdy. That is why The River Piper has the Duchin brothers as door men. No one messes with men their size! One warning is all you get. Usually the place is rocking at night with loud music and a full dance floor. And everyone enjoys a good time.

Chapter 6

It is now the second week of April, and Mayor Taylor and Civil Engineer George Hansen have traveled to St. Louis to meet with the executives of Grayson Manufacturing. There is no mistaking St. Louis with its six hundred and thirty-foot Gateway Arch. The Arch honoring Lewis and Clark's westward expansion.

St. Louis is also huge compared to Lavron, with over two million, two hundred thousand people. Grayson's Head office was not hard to find. The Mayor drove his silver Cadillac into a visitor's parking spot, took a deep breath and expressed good luck to George.

The men were met at the twin glass doors by an Intern eager to take them to a Conference room. There they met a group of nicely dressed individuals, all with bright smiles and warm handshakes. Mike Hayes the companies Chief Executive Officer offered their visitors a seat around a large Oak table. Mike then introduced Mayor Taylor and George Hansen to the rest of the committee. Coffee and water are offered. "We certainly hope your trip to our city was uneventful gentlemen?" Mike said while pouring a coffee for himself. "Thank-you Mike. Yes, it is a nice day for a drive. It has been a while since I have been to your fine city." Taylor replied. Bill Landry, Grayson's Chief

Financial Officer took over. "Well men, we have gotten wind that things got a little out of control at your Council meeting in regards to our interests. "That is correct Bill. Somehow word got out about your pending intentions. I believe it was the shortest Council meeting on record. It appears that the residents of Lavron do not want Grayson Manufacturing International to proceed with your intended project." Mayor Taylor remarked. "We have taken all of this into consideration Steven, and we are willing to enhance our offer." Bill pronounced. "We are willing to hear what Grayson is offering and we appreciate it. But if you were at the Council meeting, you would understand that our citizen's do not want change." Taylor interjected. Mike Hayes examined Taylor and Hansen. "Gentlemen, here at Grayson, we do understand that change is hard. We have been through this before, with the seven manufacturing plants in the States alone. We do not have the best reputation but, building a State-of-the-art plant in your town would be beneficial to both you and us. When I say, State-of-the-art, that means there will be literately no waste." Mike stated matter of factly. Taylor and Hansen leaned in and whispered to each other. Minutes later, George spoke up. "Bill you mentioned that you are willing to enhance your offer. What does Grayson have in mind?" Bill questioned. "Well men, we have done our homework. Mayor Taylor, in your last campaign you told the people of Lavron that a Movie Theatre and Community Centre would be built. We don't see that happening. If Grayson offered to build those facilities, and we mean the very best facilities, could that change the minds of your citizens?" Bill probed. "That is very generous of Grayson to offer such a tradeoff. And it just may be enough to sway the mindset of our residents. But they also may see it as a bribe." Taylor remarked. Bill Landry, the CFO, jumped in;

"Listen guy's, Grayson is not in the business of bribery. Think of it as a contribution in good faith to your citizen's. In return we build our plant." Bill said shrugging his shoulders. Again Mayor Steven Taylor and George Hansen turned to each other whispering. When done, the Mayor looked up and continued; "We will run this by our Council. If they vote to except your bountiful offer, we will let you know first-hand."

Taylor grinning with a gleam in his eye. "That is terrific men." Mike Hayes stated getting up from the table.

More pleasantries were expressed as everyone packed up their briefcases. Mayor Taylor and George Hansen said their good-byes with hopes to be in touch soon. Both men left thinking that this could be a good thing or a very bad thing. It is a quiet ride back to Lavron. Anxiety is setting in. "I think it's best if I call an Emergency meeting with the Council. Let's get a feel for what they say about Grayson's offer." Taylor expressed. "I couldn't agree more Steven. If they see it as a peace offering, so be it. Everyone wins." George declared. "Bill Landry did say the Theatre and Community Centre would be the best. To me that means at least three screens in the Theatre, and an Olympic size pool and basketball court in the Centre." Taylor smiled. "If that doesn't change some minds, I doubt anything will." George admitted. The two men travelled the rest of the way back to Lavron exchanging small talk. The anxiety is starting to wane. As the Mayor dropped George off at his home, the two shook hands. "I will call an Emergency meeting for tomorrow evening. Please do not mention it to anyone. Mum's the word George." Taylor pleaded. "Don't worry about me Mr. Mayor. I'll see you tomorrow." And with that George grabbed his briefcase and exited the Caddy.

The following day, Wednesday, the Lavron Herald came out. The Headlines read, "Town Council Negotiating with The Devil." Jim Lambert threw caution in the wind printing such a scathing headline. Jim being a prominent and respected figure, knew that this would rile up the citizen's. The actual piece described Grayson Manufacturing International as a bully, pushing their way through barriers to get their way. And exactly how did they get away with two polluting charges? It went on to say how the Council meeting last Thursday blew up, and how security had to shut the meeting down. The Herald also reminded the citizens of Lavron about the Council meeting this Thursday. Hopefully cooler heads will prevail, and the committee has decided against Grayson's request to build in Lavron.

That evening the members of Council met for the critical meeting. Mayor Taylor had contacted the committee secretly, telling everyone to be careful not to mention anything to anyone. When the members were seated in the chamber, the Mayor called everyone to attention. "I am sorry to have to call this meeting, and am sorry to have to call you all away from your families at this time. As you know, George Hansen and I had a meeting yesterday in St. Louis with Grayson Manufacturing." Taylor started. There is a low rumble amongst the member's, and Taylor raised his voice slightly. "Two major points were brought up. One. If Grayson were to build here in Lavron, their State-of-the-art facility would be producing no waste." More of a rumble. That is when Ward # 4 Councilor, Paul Lewis stood and asked; "Is Grayson willing to prove to us that their plant would produce no waste?" "Here, here buzzed the Chamber." George stood to answer. "Paul, my good man, this is all preliminary. Not one shovel will go into the ground until they prove that to us." Mayor Taylor then continued; "Two. If we were to grant their wish, and let the build, they would also build a Movie Theatre and Community Centre for our citizen's to enjoy," the Chamber broke in low whispers. Ward # 2 Councilor Julie Crawford then got up from her perch and pronounced; "This looks like nothing but a bribe. A company like Grayson has all the money in the world and can buy their way into places like Lavron." More here, here's from the committee. The Mayor got up once again; "Mike Hayes, Grayson's CEO calls it, a peace offering. And let me say, a Movie Theatre and Community Centre are a very nice peace offering, not to mention an expensive one."

Again, Ward # 4 Councilor, Paul Lewis jumped up and with no hesitation blurted out; "That's generous of Grayson to offer Lavron these amenities but, are you forgetting just how our population swells in the spring and summer months. This last weekend Buzz Wheeler held his annual fishing derby. Have you not noticed how the traffic has spiked? I just don't know how we could accommodate such a project." The Chamber roared with applause. The town's Civil Engineer, George Hansen then spoke above the roar; "The Grayson plant would be built on Draper Street, in the Industrial part of town. There would be plenty of room for them to place trailers in that area. Trailers to work from, and trailers for employee accommodations throughout the week. There may be a little more activity through the week, but none on weekends." That seemed to hush the Council members. "So let's just go over what we know." Stated Ward #2 Councilor Julie Crawford. "Grayson builds their State-of-the-art plant here in Lavron with the promise of no waste what so ever, and they build our Municipality, a Theatre and Community Centre as a good will gesture. If that's the case, they have my vote." A bit of a ruckus from the committee. Mayor Steven Taylor then came to his feet. "This is a major endeavor for Grayson Manufacturing and the town of Lavron. You are all in the position to change Lavron's history. If you vote yes, you will see our town prosper and thrive. If you vote no, we stay the quaint little town we have always been. It is all up to you and your vote. Each one of you fourteen members have a ballot card. Please submit your vote now." There is a pause as most took their time contemplating. Ten minutes later the poll was completed and Mayor Taylor walked over to the Ballot box and started counting the votes. Altogether there are fifteen ballots including the Mayor's. The votes went as follows; Nine for Grayson and six against. As Mayor Taylor read the Ballots, the anxiety rose once again. He expressed his appreciation for everyone's time and patience, then he read the votes. There are some remarks to the good, and some not so good, but what is done, is done. "Please go home to your families now, knowing that you have tendered a very tough obligation. We will see you all again tomorrow evening, and I pray for a more peaceful meeting." Mayor Steven Taylor conveyed. The committee shuffled out slowly. Some wondering if they really made the right choice.

Chapter 7

Thursday morning came promising to be warm and sunny. There is dew on the grass and a freshness in the air. Most of Lavron residents were either at work or on their way. Jim Lambert after printing yesterday's edition of the Herald, wanted a truthful opinion about his article. Who else to talk to but, Buzz Wheeler? Jim parked his Audi beside Buzz's pick-up truck at Lavron Lure's and made his way into the store. As soon as Jim pushed his way through the big oak door he immediately smelled the coffee brewing. "Good morning Buzz. That coffee smells good enough to drink." Jim says making his way to the counter. "Boy, you sure woke the town up with your Headlines yesterday Jim. I bet half of Lavron will be at the town meeting tonight." Buzz exclaimed as he poured Jim a cup. "I believe it was necessary to give our residents a jolt and have them realize what the Council is considering." Jim declared.

"Well Jim, if that article didn't give our citizen's a jolt, nothing will. I'm sure that the Council will reassure us tonight that Grayson Manufacturing is no longer in Lavron future, and we can all live happily ever after." Buzz remarks with a wide grin. "I hope you are right Buzz. It's like Grayson is paying some people off. Our town does not need or want them here." Jim announces. "Have no worries Jimmy, I'm sure this will be put to bed at the meeting tonight." Buzz insists sipping on his coffee. "I guess you are right. But it's the only thing on my mind these days Buzz. And that is why my article in the paper is meant to shock everyone." "Shock is the right word Jim. Like I said, I'm sure the Chamber will be full this evening and tomorrow we can go on like normal." Buzz replies. "I suppose you are right my friend. In all of my 57 years here in Lavron, I have not seen such a commotion. "Jim uttered. "Maybe it's Grayson's presence, or maybe it's because our wee town gets over crowded this time of year. But I understand your anxiety Jim." Buzz concludes. "We can expect you at the town hall tonight then?" Questions Jim. "I will be there with bells on, right after I close the shop for the day." Buzz replies. "Great! Thanks for the coffee Buzz. I better get to the office." Jim places his mug on the old wooden counter and made his way out of the store.

The residents of Lavron carry on with their work day anticipating another fiasco later on at the town meeting. There is lots of gossip among neighbors and people in grocery stores and restaurants. Citizen's chatting about the column in the Herald and what is Council thinking?

It seems that even some tourists are getting involved and asking questions. Lavron has always been the sanctuary where vacationers can relax and enjoy their time, not worrying about the hustle and bustle of everyday life. Surely, they won't change this delightful town.

As the day wore on, people gradually got off work. Most plan on dinner and then congregating at the town hall. No one really knew what to expect. They just want this issue dead and buried. A company like Grayson Manufacturing are not use to being turned down, but after last week's assembly, you would postulate that the Town Council would decline Grayson's offer.

It is still early, but the parking lot at the town hall is filling quickly. All the regular customers have arrived. Laura Rush, Jim Lambert, The Duchin twins and even Troy Laurie from the Ozark Inn are there. Everyone keeps their eyes open for Buzz. Troy Laurie has two gentlemen with him. Troy introduces the men to the people around him as guests of the Inn. They come to Lavron yearly to fish and hike. And they too want Lavron to remain the same. The crowd grows steadily. Buzz made it in the nick of time. He squeezes his way through the swarm of people and meets up with his crew just as the doors open. It is obvious that more security were hired. Everyone files in peacefully. Once in the Chamber, one would easily notice that a plexiglass barricade was also installed to protect the Council members. Once everyone is seated, the fourteen Council members cautiously and quietly take their allotted seats, followed be Mayor Steven Taylor. There is whispering amongst the audience as they wait for the meeting to come to Order. The Speaker of the House makes sure that security is in place before he calls the meeting to Order. There is total silence as Mayor Taylor stands to address the assembly. "Good evening ladies and gentlemen. We hope there will be no reoccurrence from what transpired last week. You good citizen's voted myself and my Caucus in to govern Lavron. We do not take that task lightly, and every single constituent does his or her very best." Mayor Taylor advised as he takes a sip of water. Surprisingly the hall is quiet with everybody focuses on what the Mayor has to say next, as he continues; "It seems that *Grayson* is a bad word here in Lavron. What would you say if I told you that Grayson Manufacturing International wants to work with us?"

Now the audience starts chattering. "What the Hell does that mean?" Someone shouts. "Please let me try to explain." Taylor mentions above the racket. "George Hansen and I went to St. Louis earlier this week to tell Grayson that Lavron is not interested in their proposal. They explained to us that if they did indeed build their State-of-the-art manufacturing plant here, there would be literally no waste. Then they went on to sweeten the pot."

More commotion in the stands as the Mayor went on; "Grayson has graciously offered to build our town a Movie Theatre and a Community Centre and in return we grant them their wish." Taylor said as he looks for the crowd's response. Laura Rush comes to her feet. "In your last campaign you promised that you would build those facilities Mr. Mayor." Half the spectators rise. "You are absolutely right Laura. But once we set the budget, there was just not enough revenue at this time. Grayson can fix that." Turner pleads. At that point, Ward # 2 Councilor Julie Crawford gets up. "Citizens of Lavron, please don't jump to conclusions. Grayson will build us a Theatre and Community Centre *and* they promised a waste free manufacturing plant. To your Town Council, that is a win, win." Julie then sits back down, as Buzz Wheeler stands and composes himself. "Most of our residents have been here a long time. Our population has been around six thousand for many years. Granted, we do grow immensely in the Spring and Summer months, but we are used to that because of our ability attract tourists. How would building a five hundred thousand square foot plant affect our population and our Municipality?" Buzz questions as he takes his seat. "That is a very good question Buzz. It will take two years to build such a plant. Grayson will only be allowed to enter and exit Lavron through our Industrial area. During the two years of construction, there will be more human traffic in our town but only through the week. None on weekends. Because Grayson's plant will be "State-of-the-art" when completed, they will only need a skeleton crew to run it. And the revenue from their taxes will benefit Lavron greatly." Taylor pauses for another drink of water as the audience chatted among themselves. Then he resumed his dialogue; "We will carry on with meetings and negotiations with Grayson, but let me reassure you, the Movie Theatre and Community Centre will be completed before we allow their plant to open." Finally, a few cheers and yeas from the crowd. It seems as though Mayor Taylor has gotten through to his citizens. Well, most of them anyway….

Ten minutes later, the meeting is dismissed and everyone gets up to leave. On the way out, big Brock Duchin declares, free drinks at the Pickled Piper for those who would like to talk about Grayson's proposal.

Thursday nights are always busy at the Pickled Piper. At nine o'clock a disc jockey sparks up his turn tables and cranks up the music. The dance floor gets crowded and the beverages get flowing. The Duchin brothers, Brock and Greg are the first to arrive at the Piper. Brock informs Maddie the bar maid that a bunch of people will be showing up for free drinks. "Are you crazy Brock? You know how busy we get on Thursday nights!" States Maddie. "I will monitor the drinks Maddie, you just pour them.

I feel the need to talk about Grayson's pending scheme and I will pay for the drinks." Brock insisted. A minute later a line of patrons file through the door looking for free cocktails and any information regarding Grayson Manufacturing. Greg and Brock stand at the oak bar. They are big men. Linebackers. They count at least forty people that were at the town hall. Brock goes over to the D.J. and asks him to lower the volume. "I'm glad you all came. Please get yourself a drink." Brock announces. When everyone is content and sipping on their beverage, Brock then speaks up." "Two weeks ago our town was looking forward to the fishing season and the influx of vacationers. Today we find ourselves in the hands of corporate bribery. I believe Grayson is nothing but a wolf in sheep's clothing!

Building a Movie Theatre and Community Centre is chicken feed to a company like Grayson. There has to be another reason they want the land on Draper Street. Jefferson City is only eighty miles up the road. I realize the taxes would be more expensive there, but then again, chicken feed." Brock expresses sincerely. Jim Lambert speaks above the group. "To me it looks like Grayson, has Mayor Taylor and George Hansen, as well as the rest of the Council in the palm of their hands. I bet we will find out next week that, it's a done deal!" There are boo's throughout the tavern. Trish Burns, a local Flower shop owner waits for a pause, then stands and yells out; "I don't know much about politics, but when was the last time you went to a movie or went for a swim? If Grayson wants to build their monster plant with the promises of no waste, why not let them build us those facilities as well? I would love to see a Theatre and Community Centre here in Lavron!" Trish says blushing when the room started buzzing. Arguments start. Greg Duchin has to break up a shoving match between a couple of patrons while others try to get the last word in, in their disagreement. Laura Rush, Buzz Wheeler and Jim Lambert sit in a booth and go over the pro's and con's about Grayson's proposal. No one can get their head around it. It is just too much to absorb all at once. It appears that nothing really gets resolved, and the Disc Jockey eventually turns the music back up. Some of the gang that came for a free drink stay, but most weren't in the mood to celebrate, and left.

Chapter 8

The following day more vacationer's come. The Ozark Inn is to capacity, as are the other two Motels in Lavron. To Troy and Traci Laurie it's like a revolving door. Tourist's came in as others leave. But that's what puts food on the table. One of Inn's guests is a photographer from out of State. All that Troy knows is that his camera is made by Canon, and his lens is almost a foot long. Del Phillips is here in Lavron to do an exclusive photo shoot of Missouri's fowl. Missouri is home to over four hundred species of birds and it seems like they all congregate here in Lavron and Lake of the Ozark's. It is a perfect setting for these birds, not only because of the water but the trees as well. Different types of Pine trees, White Oak and Flowering Dogwood trees make good shelters, and provide berries to eat.

Del is packing his car for the day when Troy saunters over. "Be sure to set a few pictures aside for us to display, will you Mr. Phillips?" Troy asked. "Please call me Del, and of course I will give you a few copies. I will probably take a thousand pics today alone." Del said, patting his camera. "By the way, what is happening here? Rumor has it that some big Auto Parts company wants to build a massive plant in Lavron. Does that make any sense? Del questioned. "Apparently it makes sense to Grayson Manufacturing International. They say that Lavron is centralized for distribution throughout the States, and we have the land available." Troy declared shaking his head. "This is only the second time I've been to Lavron. It is beautiful here. I would hate to see it change." Del remarked. "You and me both Del, you and me both. Grayson is relentless though. They have offered to build Lavron a Theatre and Community Centre as a good will gesture." Troy mentions.

"Good will gesture? Sounds like a bribe to me. A Theatre and Community Centre is a drop in the bucket to a huge company like that." Del states. "I hear you Del. Some may call it a bribe. Other's may call it progress. All I know is that, it's out of our hands now, and up to the Big Wigs." Troy pronounces. "I just hope that if and when I come back, that your little town hasn't changed." Del reflects as he got into his Volvo. "Thanks Del. You have a nice day now." Troy comments as he walks back to the office. His wife Traci is behind the desk straightening pamphlets regarding hiking trails and bird Sanctuaries, when Troy opens the screen door. "The word sure has gotten out about Grayson. Two of our guests came with me last night to the Town meeting, and the Photographer I was just chatting with, heard about some big company moving into the area." Troy utters.

"News travels fast Troy. I believe even the Tourist's do not want Lavron to change." Traci adds. "I'm thinking that maybe we should get a bunch of us town folk together, and have our own little meeting about Grayson Manufacturing." Troy blurts. "I don't know what that would prove but, at least you would get a consensus on how our resident's feel about this issue." Traci suggests. "I will make some phone calls. I am sure that Buzz Wheeler would gladly hold a private meeting in his Storage room sometime next week." Troy mentions scrolling through his phone.

Over the course of the weekend Troy gets hold of all the usual suspects. Jim Lambert, Laura Rush, Greg and Brock Duchin, Buzz Wheeler and even Maddie Thompson, the Bar Maid from the River Piper. They are all to meet on Tuesday evening after hours in Buzz's storage room at the back of Lavron Lure's. Everyone seems stoked to have a clandestine meeting regarding their town's future. Buzz even offers to supply coffee and cake.

Del Phillips, the out of State Photographer steps into the Ozark Inn's office. He brings with him a file folder. "Good morning Mrs. Laurie. I told your husband that I would drop off some pictures from yesterday's excursion. I hope you like them." Del says placing the folder on the desk. "That is too kind of you." Traci remarks reaching for the pics. "These are terrific pics Mr. Phillips. You must have a powerful lens, being able to get such close-ups. I will get Troy to frame some of these pictures and we'll display them right here in the office." Traci announces with a big smile. "I appreciate that. Thank-you. And before I depart, I wish only the very best for your quaint Village. I would hate to see this piece of paradise change." Del mentions being sincere. "That is nice of you to say that, Mr. Phillips." Traci replies crossing her fingers. "Next year I will bring my family with me and try our hand at fishing." Del declares as he waved good-bye.

Tuesday evening couldn't come fast enough. As promised, Buzz has coffee and some kind of marble cake on a card table in his Storage room, ready for consumption. Everyone shows up on time not knowing what to expect. Buzz welcomes the group; "Please help yourselves to coffee and cake. Troy, you called this meeting. What is on your mind beside the obvious?" Buzz questions. Troy, looking uneasy, stared at his peers shaking his head. "There is something fishy about Grayson wanting the land on Draper Street. There are plenty of other places they could purchase that kind of acreage. They are willing to build a Movie Theatre and Community Centre in Lavron just to get their hands on that property. Like I said, something's fishy." Troy announces still shaking his head. "You've got a point there Troy. I hadn't thought of that before," states Jim Lambert. Big Greg Duchin then stood up.

"Brock and I are going to take a drive down to Draper Street. I doubt we will find anything worth reporting, but you never know. Half of that land isn't even cleared." "Great idea Greg," remarked Laura Rush. "If you need the old surveys, I can retrieve them from the Library." "I don't think that is necessary at this point Laura, but thanks for the heads up." Greg states. Buzz then looks at Maddie Thompson. "Glad you could make it Maddie. I didn't realize that you are a rebel." Buzz said jokingly. "I am here in support of my boy's." Maddie pronounces, locking her arms around Greg and Brock Duchin's. "Good to hear that Maddie. Lavron may need all the support it can get.

Greg and Brock, you guy's take that drive to Draper Street and snoop around. In the meantime, I suggest we wait to see what Grayson and our Town Council come up with. And hopefully it's nothing." Buzz notes. The gang then finished their coffee and cake, while making small talk. They leave the store secretly, hoping not to be seen.

Greg and Brock decides to get up early the next morning and explore Draper Street before they went to work. The early morning sun in April is welcome. The guy's grab coffee and muffins at the MacDonald's drive-thru in. Greg's beat up Toyota Corolla is barely big enough to fit both men, but they manage. Ten minutes later they turn onto Draper Street. It's a long road with factories and office buildings scattered in no particular order. The brother's drive slowly until they come to the land in question.

Greg pulls his car over to the side of the road, puts it in park and gets out with his coffee. They look around trying to imagine a five hundred thousand square foot building on this property. "I didn't know how big twelve acres is." Brock observes, while watching where he is walking. "It's a lot of room and half of it is still covered with trees and shrubs." Greg replies. "It won't take long to clear this land. Let's take a stroll to the back of the property. Maybe Grayson knows of a buried treasure back there." Brock said, punching Greg's shoulder. "You punch like a girl. Just like your playing days" Greg states with a grin as the twin's make their way to the back edge. The trees and bushes are thick in spots and most of the shrubs have thorns, but the guys persevere. When they get to the edge of the property, it opened up to tall grass. The Duchin brothers could hear flowing water. They paced no more than sixty feet when they came upon the mighty Osage river. The Osage river is a tributary off of the Missouri river, but still one of the main rivers in Missouri. It is wide and one can feel the roar, as the water rushed by. "Are you thinking what I'm thinking Greg? Is this why Grayson wants this land?" Brock asks, wondering. "I don't understand. Grayson said that there would be literally no waste from their "State-of-the-art" plant." Greg mentions. "No waste means, no solid waste as well as no emissions. I can't see any large manufacturing plant not producing some sort of waste." Brock stated as he took a few pictures with his phone. "We better let Buzz and the rest of the group know what we have discovered." Greg replied. "You know, I actually forgot that the river flowed through this part of town. It's kind of hidden back here." Mentions Brock. "Exactly!" Greg blurts, then continued; "We will let the gang know about this, but in the meantime, we have a new fishing spot brother." With mixed feelings the guy's explored the area until they had to leave for work. When they got back to Greg's car, Draper Street was alive with traffic. "This street will be quite busy if Grayson gets their way.

Can you imagine building a massive plant, with only one access into this part of town?" Brock queries. "That is the least of our worries bud. I think I will stop in at the Herald office at noon and let Jim know about our discovery." Greg states. "Good idea Greg. He won't take this lightly."

Later on that morning, four executives from Grayson Manufacturing International, four Council members from Lavron, as well as the Minister of the Environment, the Honorable Herb Turner, meets the Council members of Lavron's town hall. Mayor Steven Taylor welcomes everyone to the town and offers coffee, tea and pasties to all. Once the committee are settled around the large pine table, the meeting began. "We are delighted that you were available to attend our meeting, Mr. Turner." States George Hansen. "Thank-you Mr. Hansen. When I got word of this meeting, I cleared my schedule. Grayson Manufacturing are not strangers to us." Herb declared staring at both Mike Hayes and Bill Landry. Mike then got up and pronounces; "The big question in all of these negotiations is not finances, nor zoning or permits, nor timing and traffic, but waste! We, at Grayson are planning to build in Lavron, a State-of-the -art manufacturing plant with little to no waste. The waste that is produced, will be put in fifty gallon drums and shipped to a safe facility." Mike then sits down, clearly showing some frustration. Cheryl Quinn, Lavron's City Attorney, slowly gets up from her seat focusing on two depositions. "Mr. Hayes, Grayson Manufacturing has been charged twice for polluting waterways in Philadelphia and in Oregon. And we happen to know both times Grayson somehow had the charges reduced or dropped. We asked Herb Turner to be present today so that Lavron will not have to deal with that issue. Our land and waterways are what brings tourists and angler's here, and that is all part of Lavron's livelihood."

Bill Landry, Grayson's CFO, rises and states; "This proposed project is a massive undertaking. I will personally see to it that Grayson sends a monthly statement to Herb Turner's office regarding any waste and or emissions produced. Right now we need to roll up our sleeves and work out the financial details, for the twelve acres on Draper Street." The nine-person committee then focuses on the paperwork in front of them. There is very little bickering about the money involved. The group works hand in hand to get specific factors worked out. At noon they break for lunch as the Minister of the Environment, Herb Turner excuses himself, siting that he is no longer needed. Mayor Taylor has arranged a catering service. Sandwiches, wraps, drinks and dessert are on offer. After everyone has enough to eat, the group works tirelessly all afternoon banging out different but important details. By early evening it appears that most of the negotiations are complete.

The lawyers would make sure the T's are crossed and the I's dotted. It was a long day for everyone and exhausting as well. Before the committee packed up their briefcases, Bill mentions; "I thought it would be fitting to let you and your Council know, Mayor Taylor, that Grayson has already inquired and has asked for quotes regarding a Movie Theatre with a pair of screens, and Community Centre with a hotel sized pool and a Basketball Court. We have three companies working on that as we speak. Grayson's hope, is that the two facilities would be suitable to your town's liking?" "Thank-you Bill. It is generous of Grayson to offer such amenities to our little community. I'm sure all the members of Council will be thrilled about your magnificent contribution." Taylor declares. "Our pleasure, Mr. Mayor. All in the name of fair business and fair trade." Bill remarked. The group then slowly get up from their chairs, pack their briefcases, and have a good stretch. After handshakes and good will gestures, everyone bid good-bye, for now.

At noon that same day, Greg drops by the Herald office to chat with Jim. He climbed the six stairs to the one story building and opened the glass door to the office. Jim's Administration Assistant, Lori Baldwin greeted Greg with a smile and asked him how she could help. "Yes, I'm here to see Jim." Greg said returning the smile. "Down the hall, first door on the right. I will let Jim know you are here Greg." Lori replied as she watched the big man walk down the hallway. Jim's door is open. "Come on in Greg. I haven't seen you since last night. What's up? Jim questioned offering Greg a chair. "This won't take long Jim. Brock and I went to the property on Draper Street this morning. At first it looked like any other lot. Half of it is bare, the other half full of trees and bushes, and is quite dense. When we made it to the end of the plot, it opened up to tall grass and we could hear water flowing. We followed our ears and found the Osage river, sixty feet away," declared Greg, looking for Jim's response. "Those Bastards! I knew there was some reason Grayson wanted that land. Now we know. I doubt the river is even on the survey's." Jim remarks pounding his fist on his desk. "Well Jim, I thought we had better let you know. I'm sure you will tell the others what we found. But at this point, I don't think there is anything else we can do." Greg added getting up from his seat. "True enough Greg. Thanks for letting me know. I will let everyone involved know what you guy's discovered. If Grayson's plans are to secretly pollute our rivers, they have another thing coming." Jim mentioned as he got up from his desk. He gazed out his office window at the picturesque scenery, then stated; "Come on Greg, I'll buy you some lunch. It looks like you are starving," the two men wandered out of the Herald office and jumped into their own vehicles. Greg followed Jim to Hungry Hank's, All You Can Eat restaurant. Once inside, Jim spotted Trish Burns, the owner of Blooms. Blooms is one of two flower shops in Lavron.

Jim excused himself from Greg momentarily, and went over to Trish's table. In the couple of minutes Jim was conversing with Trish, her demeanor went from carefree, to worrisome. Jim seems to be spreading the word.

Chapter 9

Months have now past. It is the beginning of August and Lavron has gone about it's business as usual. All the talk about Grayson Manufacturing has died down, and both plots of land have been cleared. The property on Draper Street was much easier to clear, than the lot set aside for the Theatre and Community Centre. It required a little blasting to level out that particular piece of land. But both properties sit bare for the time being. Construction will commence in September. That was one of the stipulations Council invoked, as Lavron is too busy with vacationers/ tourists etc. until then.

Buzz Wheeler has had a very busy few months. He hired a couple of students, so that he could offer live bait and a cleaning service. For two dollars a fish, Lavron Lure's will clean all the fish you can catch. Larry Anderson is one of the students responsible for selling bait and cleaning the fish. He is a short, stocky sixteen-year-old. Over the last two months he has cleaned hundreds of fish. Stepping in through the side door, Larry asks; "Hey Buzz, how quickly do fish reproduce?" Buzz had to think for a second."I don't really know Larry. I would guess that they reproduce annually. Why do you ask?" Buzz queried. "I bet I have cleaned close to three hundred fish so far this summer. And thats just me. There have been thousands of anglers out on, Lake of the Ozark's this season. Everyone wants to catch their limit, and even if they don't, that's still a lot of fish. I bet the lake gets pretty depleted by Autumn." Larry suggested. "We haven't had any issue with the fish population yet Larry. Don't forget that the Lake is, sixty-one thousand square miles in circumference, and is one hundred, forty feet deep in some spots. That's a lot of space for a lot of fish. If we ever lost the fish, we would also lose our tourist industry, and we don't want that." Reflected Buzz.

It is getting to be the Dog days of summer. In the afternoon, the temperature reaches ninety degrees. Most of the people that want to fish, go early in the morning or after the sun sets. The few restaurants and bars that are in town are packed. Air conditioning is key, as residents and vacationers want to enjoy a cool beverage in a cool establishment. The River Piper is the most popular bar for the younger crowd, and the Elk's Hangout is famous for its wild fishing and hunting stories, with an older populace. Both taverns have a friendly staff and will do what they can to keep their customers happy. Every once in a while though, a patron with one too many drinks, will cause problems. This happens in every bar, but in Lavron if you cause issues, you will no longer be welcome. This policy has worked for generations. Greg and Brock Duchin are Doormen at the River Piper in the evenings, and have been since they left University. They are worried that when the construction begins on Draper Street, there will be problems at night. A lot of workers, away from their families throughout the week, want to let loose at night, and that usually leads to physicality. For this reason, the River Piper has installed cameras in the parking lot, and as you walk in the front door. The few times when there has been an altercation and someone gets hurt, it's a long drive to the Hospital in Jefferson City. Lavron has a Walk -in -Clinic and Treatment Center, but no Hospital.

Greg and Brock enjoy working at the Piper. The people that know them, envy them. After all they did play for SLU for four years. Very few patron's cause problems when the brothers are on the door, because of their sheer size, but every once in a while some drunk feels the need to challenge. It doesn't usually work out the way they want, hence the Hospital in Jefferson City.

Some people still refer to Lavron as a Village. Most of those people grew up here, and refuse to admit that Lavron has become a Town. It is a picturesque Borough, with rolling hills, gorgeous landscapes, mature trees, streams, creeks, rivers and lakes. The Tourist Information Center is the place to go for any particular advice, guidance or direction you may need. The Center is a log cabin and is maintained beautifully. The staff plant different flowers around the small cabin to brighten up the surroundings, and the inside looks like Davey Crockett lived there. Pine logs, a foot in diameter placed on top of each other, gives the place an authentic feel. There are posters of all the different species of bird and fish in the area, and pamphlets, free for the taking. It is also the place to go for maps of the hiking trails, and of course, souvenirs. Megan Fournier is a Sophomore at Lincoln University in Jefferson City. The nineteen-year-old is studying Botany. Growing up in Lavron, Megan has always loved the Flora, but is more interested in things like Algae, Fungi, Mosses and Ferns.

When not working at the Tourist Center, she is off collecting samples for her own personal observations. When she graduates, Megan wants to become either a Field Botanist or an Aquatic Biologist. The region around Lavron would welcome someone with a degree of that nature. Megan's main concern, from the side studies she has performed, is that, Lake of the Ozark's is not as clean as it once was. Algae has been growing at an unnatural rate. Her studies, dating back only three years, suggests that phosphates and possible fertilizers have boosted the growth of the organism. Some phosphates occur naturally when the oxygen levels in the water are low, but the growth rate of these algaes would indicate that toxins have been introduced. It is something that should be monitored carefully.

Building Grayson's State-of-the-art manufacturing plant is a massive undertaking. Mike Hayes, Bill Landry and one of Grayson's Engineers, Steve Wilson are at the Draper Street site to meet with the owner of Fox Construction and his appointed Site Foreman. Fox Construction has won the contract to build Grayson's newest location. When completed, the Lavron Site will be centralized for better distribution throughout the States, and will take some of the manufacturing burden away from the other seven Plants across America. The three Grayson executives got to the Site early to take a look around. The land had already been cleared, so it didn't take the men long to explore the surroundings. Sixty feet from the property line, they found the Osage River. That is where the biggest conversation took place. The three are in deep discussion when a white Ford pick-up truck with Fox Con. painted on the doors pulls up. The Grayson Board members trudge back to meet with owner, Glen Fox and Site Foreman, Pete Hawkins. After introductions and handshakes, Steve Wilson opens some drawings of the future Plant. The five men talk about staging and time frames. And they talk about permits and supervision. They agree that no more than forty workers would be on the Site at any given time. That was another stipulation from Town Council. After lengthy dialogue, the guy's take a walk around the area and find themselves by the river. The rushing water flows rapidly over rocks and fallen trees. The river at that point is at least ten feet deep and will sweep anyone away, should they fall in. As the men sauntered back to their vehicles, Mike Hayes took Glen Fox aside. "Glen, it certainly looks like everything is ready begin. We at Grayson are happy that Fox Construction has the competence and capability to build such an immense and complicated project. There is just one more thing we would like to inquire about." Mike stated, staring directly into Glen's eyes. "And what would that be Mike?" Questioned Glen. "We were wondering if you would be interested in a side project?"

Chapter 10

There was quite a gathering on Draper Street. Mayor Taylor, George Hansen and most of the town's Council were there with the dignitaries from Grayson Manufacturing. Mike Hayes and Mayor Taylor were holding silver spades. A photographer from the Herald along with Jim Lambert were covering the ground breaking event. There were a few dozen citizen's here to witness the affair including the group that met in Buzz's storage room. Both Grayson's CEO and Lavron's Mayor plunged their spades into the soil in unison. There were smiles and handshakes as Steven Taylor declared a Historic day in Lavron. "We are pleased to welcome Grayson Manufacturing International to our Municipality. Grayson has made it possible for Lavron to prosper, and has graciously awarded us with a Movie Theatre and Community Center. We are delighted to partner with such a respected firm and will work hand in hand to make their endeavor successful." Taylor stated. The applause was almost nonexistent. Buzz wandered over to Jim who was writing in his day-timer. "So Jim, how are you going to document this event? Will it be a Historic day or the beginning of the end?" Buzz inquired, giving Jim a nudge. "At this point it would be hard to crucify Grayson. They are Devil's in sheep's clothing. Everyone is thrilled about the Theatre and Center, so to make them look like bandits would give the wrong impression. We will have to wait to dig up dirt on them," remarked Jim. "I suppose you are right Jim. Time will tell. We'll keep tabs on these guys' and what transpires after this mammoth project," voiced Buzz as they walked slowly to their vehicles. Most of the crowd had dispersed and the Grayson executives left in their black Lincoln Town cars.

Draper Street will be very busy. The heavy equipment will be moving in shortly, as well as the steel girders and I- beams. A drilling truck will auger down thirty feet to put the footings in place. From there it's full steam ahead. At the back of the property, Grayson will stage many trailers. Some of these trailers will be housing for the employees throughout the week, and a couple will be strictly to work out of. Grayson will also provide a stationary food truck to prevent the workers from going into town. The Site Foreman, Pete Hawkins will be here first thing tomorrow morning to make sure things are put where they need to be. Most of the construction crew will be coming in from the St. Louis area and will stay here through the week. It will take four or five days to get everything set up and be fully functional. Grayson awarded Fox Construction the contract, as they have a reputation for doing a good job that is on time and within budget.

The other construction site on the East side of Lavron will be built by another reputable company. The Theatre and Community Center won't take as long to build, barring no delays, and should be open for business this time next year.

A siren was heard across town. The Lavron Fire Department summon their volunteer force with a siren and an alert on their phone. With only two Fire trucks in the vicinity, it didn't take long to man the vehicles. With seven men to a truck, they are usually rolling out of the Station within minutes. Smoke was reported coming from the Town Hall. Ten minutes after the alert, the first truck was ready to roll, but by the time they arrive at the Municipal building, flames could be seen peering through the roof. Volunteer Firefighters grabbed hoses as quickly as possible and hooked them up to the hydrants. To battle the blaze, Voluntary Chief, Dwayne Parsons climbed a ladder on the truck with an unwilling hose. The heat was threatening as he blasted water into the inferno. Black smoke billowed out of the burning building.

The second Firetruck got to the scene minutes later and was strategically placed in a position to help fight the raging fire. Four hoses rushed water onto and into the establishment. The volunteers worked tirelessly, trying their best to contain the fire, but it was futile. The fire must have been burning long before anyone noticed. It seemed that all they could do is just keep dousing the flames with high pressure water. Three hours after arriving, the Firemen declared the fire was out. The whole back half of the two story building was destroyed. A fire like that doesn't just happen, and an investigation would be required to find the cause. Bystander's couldn't believe what they have witnessed. Dwayne Parsons spotted Mayor Taylor standing with other members of Council behind a band of Caution tape. He had tears streaming down his cheeks. "We are terribly sorry this has happened Mayor Taylor. An investigation will determine how it got started. Fowl play is what I suspect." Dwayne gestured. "Thank-you Dwayne. Thank God no one was hurt. Obviously your men have been trained properly and they deserve all our gratitude. I have put a call in to the Town Works. They will be here momentarily to barricade the surroundings with portable metal fencing, that will secure the area. Please take your men to the River Piper for a decent meal and a couple of brews. I will personally pick up the tab," stated Taylor.

The Lavron Herald's Photographer was having a busy day. Buck Fendley had just gotten the photos from the Draper Street ground breaking developed, when he heard the sirens. He called over to the Station but received no answer, so he grabbed his camera, ran out to his Jeep and drove the four blocks to the Fire Station just as the first truck was leaving.

Buck followed the Emergency vehicle to the scene. He darted to spot a where he could get some good shots while staying out of the way of the Fire Team. The fire was spreading. Flames hurtled ten feet into the air above the roof. News travels fast in a small town. Within an hour, hundreds of citizen's watched in horror as their Town Hall burned. It wouldn't take long for the gossip and rumors to begin. This was another trait of a small town. Hours later, Buck Fendley finished taking the last couple of pictures of the scarred building. He would drop the hundreds of proofs off for developing in the Dark Room before checking in with Jim Lambert. Jim would want a fully detailed description of what Buck and the Firefighter's experienced. By now they must have had an idea of when the fire started. Both Jim and Buck headed over to the Piper to interview some of the Volunteer Firefighters, but they had to wait to hear from Dwayne Parsons first. Dwayne would fill out a detailed report about the incident and send it to the Fire Marshall's office in Jefferson City. From there, an investigation will be launched. Investigations got underway quickly when fowl play is suspected.

By the time the Fire Crew got the equipment and themselves cleaned up, the sun was setting. Although the men were tired, they are looking forward to a bite to eat and a few of beers at the River Piper. Not all of the Volunteers could make it, but when the dozen or so men walked through the door of the Pub, a standing ovation greeted them. The Piper was packed and everyone wanted to shake the hands of today's heroes. Maddie Thompson was trying to keep up with the drinks and the kitchen was understaffed this evening. Jim and Buck were getting different points of view from various witnesses and Firefighters, but Jim noticed something was amiss. Brock and Greg Duchin were nowhere to be seen. Employed at the Town Works during the day, the guys would surely know what happened this afternoon. Jim sauntered over to Maddie who was uncapping one beer after another. "Maddie, I guess having a fire in town is good for business?" Jim asked. "Too good Jim. I'm having a hard time keeping up," replied Maddie.

"I have been here interviewing some of the Firemen, and basically anyone that can tell me what they believed happened, when I noticed that the Duchin boys were not here." Jim stated. "I noticed that as well Jimmy. They were supposed to be here two hours ago. Greg called and said that something had come up and that they will be late." Maddie remarked pouring a draught. "Something big must have come up for them to be two hours late," offered Jim. "Normally I would tell them to take the night off but, as you can see, we are quite busy," voiced Maddie.

Ten minutes later the two men in question march through the Piper's front door. The guys took a look around and spotted Maddie frantically trying to manage the drink orders. "Sorry we are late Mad. Greg's Corolla broke down and by the time we figured out what was wrong, and found the proper part, time took over." Brock announced while snapping open a couple of tall Bud Light cans. "Well I'm glad you guys are here now Brock. It must have been a messy job fixing Greg's car. Your fingernails are filthy and you smell like smoke." Maddie retorted.

Buck and Jim tracked down Greg as he was delivering a couple plates of chicken wings to a side table. "We know you are busy Greg. We're just wondering if you heard anything different about the fire this afternoon?" queried Jim. "Wish I could help you out guys. Brock and I were trying to fix that piece of junk out there in the parking lot. Ended up taking two hours off of work as well." Greg remarked. "Ok buddy, we thought that you, and or Brock might have heard something, anything, because the whole thing smells fishy," pronounced Jim as he detected a hint of smoke.

Chapter 11

The Fire Marshall and his crew were in Lavron early the following day. Arriving at the scene, they know that investigating a fire was a step by step process. Dwayne Parsons greeted the Fire Marshall, Bill Shannon with coffee for his group, and the keys to the burnt building. The two shook hands as Bill explained to Dwayne how the team would proceed with the investigation. "We will go in from the front and slowly work our way to where the fire began. At this point we have no idea if it was the furnace or electrical or other." Bill mentioned. "You do not want to rule out fowl play Bill. That is my gut feeling," stated Dwayne. "That would come under the heading of *other*, and we will not rule out anything. I am very confident in my staff. They will go through the place with a fine tooth comb," announced Bill. He then called his crew over and opened up the Blueprints of the building that he had printed earlier. "As you all know, safety is key. Wear your personal protective equipment at all times. We will enter from the front of the building and work our way back. Leave no stone unturned.

The structure may very well be compromised, so again I can't stress safety enough," warned Bill. The group of four including the Marshall put on their PPE, clicked on their headlamps and slowly entered the premises. The front of the building was unharmed except for the smell of smoke. As the crew worked their way through, it was obvious that most of the damage was where the Town Council meet.

The wide open expanse was black with soot. The chairs and huge table are burnt beyond repair, the carpet and curtains were gone, the light fixtures melted. At this point the team started to think that this was no accident. Bill told his men to check the furnace and electrical rooms. When it was discovered that the fire did not originate in those rooms, the team quickly started to look for signs of arson. Using different chemical compounds, the Fire team locate an area near the Janitorial room that had evidence of an accelerant. This was where the fire started and spread quickly. They determined that more than five gallons of gas was poured throughout that room and into the Chamber. Now that they knew this fire was started purposely, the team looked for fingerprints, footprints and a means of entry. To their dismay it was discovered that the way the culprit or culprits got into the building was through a window the Firefighter's broke to get their hoses in position to fight the blaze. No fingerprints were found on the window and it was very hard to tell if the Perps broke the lock or the Fire crew. Certainly the Volunteer Firemen would be interviewed. No jerry can or any container that held the gasoline was found. This was a well thought out caper. The Fire Marshall's team worked patiently for another three hours but no foot or fingerprints were found. They knew the fire was an act of arson, yet no other evidence could be retrieved.

In other cases, when little to no evidence is collected, the team tries to thinks of motive. Who and why would someone or someones do such a thing? The Lavron Police would have a better idea about the reason behind this. They knew very well that the town's residents were upset with the Town Council agreeing with an alleged corrupt corporation to purchase land here. Some still see the Theatre and Community Center as a bribe. There were a handful of people that stood out as being completely against Grayson Manufacturing moving into Lavron. The things were, all of the citizen's that were against Grayson, were prominent and well respected residents. The police know that Buzz

Wheeler, Jim Lambert and Laura Rush, as well as Troy Laurie and the Duchin twins were in cahoots with one another. Jim Lambert published an edition of the Herald condemning Grayson Manufacturing. Some of their feelings bordered on hatred, but to take matters in their own hands was insane. This investigation may be futile though. With little to no evidence, the only thing the police could look into was if everyone had an alibi. And anyone planning a crime of this magnitude would surely have an alibi.

PART 2

Chapter 12

Twenty months have now past. Lavron has shaped up nicely. The citizens have enjoyed the newly opened Movie Theatre and it seems that teenage kids have taken ownership of the Basketball Court in the Community Center. The town became peaceful. The Town Hall was rebuilt and the mega project on Draper Street was nearing completion. The Grayson Manufacturing plant is massive. The plant itself is five stories high where the warehouse is located, and two stories where the actual manufacturing will take place. The building takes up most of the twelve acres, allowing just enough space for parking. Grayson planned to have a Ribbon cutting ceremony in a month from now.

Despite all the turbulence the town residents caused at the beginning, the construction had gone on smoothly. The construction crews had been polite and courteous when they came into town for dinner and or drinks, and the citizens had been friendly for the most part. Mayor Taylor could not have been happier. The horrendous fire at the Hall was now in the past and although no one was ever charged in the arson case, the building had been restored to its former self. The people of Lavron now have a Theatre, pool and Basketball court to entertain themselves. Grayson even allowed for a fair sized Conference room. That took the pressure off of Taylor to find room in the budget for such an expensive and extravagant undertaking.

The Osage river behind the new plant had been kept confidential. The Duchin brothers had beaten down a new path to the river, away from the construction site. The guys had an ulterior motive for doing that. They figured that they could go fishing, and keep an eye on Grayson, to ensure they are not doing anything shady. The fishing was terrific! Every time the boys came out to the river, they came home with their limit. Today was no different. As the guys stood on the river bank, it seemed as though a fish was brought in with every other cast. Brock decided to move down the bank to a new location just for a change of scenery. On the far edge of Grayson's property, Brock noticed a three-foot-wide track stemming from the plant and leading to the river. It wouldn't have been noticeable if it wasn't for the tall grass being trampled. "Greg, get over here!" Brock yelled. "What is it?" Greg asked as he saunters over to where Brock was standing. "Take a look at this. For some reason there is a path from the plant to the river," declared Brock. "This could be where the construction crew dumped unwanted soil, but that should have been taken away by truck," stated Greg.

"I think that we should ask the Site Foreman why this track is here." Brock insisted. "Good call bro," remarked Greg. The brothers decided to come back the following day and grill the Site Foreman on why this pathway was necessary. The Foreman could tell the twins to, *go take a hike,* but their size usually bought them some respect.

Early the next morning Greg and Brock stopped and bought coffee. They wanted to get over to the work site before the men started work and before they had to be at their jobs. It was just before 7 am. The guys pulled up to a trailer where the Foreman, Pete Hawkins and Engineer, Steve Wilson worked from. The twenty-eight-foot trailer was weather beaten and dirty. It certainly had seen better days. Greg went up the five steps to the rear door and gave it a couple firm taps. A couple of seconds passed before the door swungs open. "Hello guy's." Pete says with a confused look on his face. "Good morning, I take it that you would be the Site Foreman?" Greg inquired. "That's correct. What can I do for you gents?" questioned Pete. "I am Greg Duchin and this is my brother Brock. We are just a couple of concerned residents from Lavron," stated Greg.

Hawkins thought, *what do these clowns want.* "Come in for a minute men. How can I help you?" "Brock and I were out here fishing yesterday. We noticed that there is a track running from the back of the plant to the river. Our question is, why?" Greg locked eyes with Pete. "Well guys, quite frankly that is none of your business. But, before you make a Federal case out of it, let me explain. In a State-of-the-art facility such as this one, there will be water running through the different milling and casting machinery for cooling purposes. That water will be filtered and sent to the river. And believe me, that water will be tested frequently for any contamination. A report must be sent monthly to the Environmental Minister," Pete clarifies. "Ok, Mr. Foreman, thank-you for your honesty. We thought that Grayson was trying to do something culpable," replied Greg. "Let me assure you men that Grayson has gone above and beyond, to make this mega project impeccable and precise. Believe me when I say, they keep their thumb on me at all times." Pete remarked with a frown. "Sorry for taking up your time sir. Thanks for clearing that up for us," voiced Brock. The men then shook hands and bid farewell.

The guys left the Site satisfied with what Pete Hawkins exclaimed. It seemed perfectly logical to channel the castoff water to the river provided it is within Government regulations. Greg and Brock headed to work, but had to stop to buy some breakfast on the way. April was a very busy month when working for the Town. On top of the regular duties such as garbage detail, the Department had seasonal jobs to do. Storm sewers needed to be cleared for proper drainage, road and sidewalk repairs were needed, as well as tree maintenance and grass cutting.

If you landed a job with the Town, you had employment for life. The Duchin brothers are well liked. Not only were they good, reliable workers, but they could lift a ton as well. They had been assigned to lay patio and unilock stones leading up to and around the newly opened Community Center. It was hard work, but the boy's love being outside and talking to the locals.

Buzz's fishing derby was just around the corner. The fishing season was opening next weekend as was his tournament. This year was no different. Angler's from all around were expected to arrive in Lavron and the neighboring area to participate. The residents had already noticed the influx of visitors. The Motels in the town were beginning to fill up. The Campgrounds around Lavron were a little slower, as the nights were still quite chilly. Troy and Traci Laurie of the Ozark Inn are busy getting ready for the season. They are expecting to see Del Phillips and a guest today. He had made a reservation a month ago for a three-night stay. "I wonder if Mr. Phillips will be bringing his camera or his fishing rod this year?" Traci probed. "Well Honey, I wouldn't be surprised if he brings both," stated Troy jokingly. The husband and wife team continued cleaning the main office and made sure that the pictures Del gave them two years before were dusted and straightened. When Del finally comes through the screen door, it is nearing 3 pm. and he has someone in tow. "Traci and Troy. How good to see you both," declared Del. "Hello Mr. Phillips. It's been a while." Traci remarked with a wide smile. Troy rushed over and shook Del's hand. "And who do we have here, Mr. Phillips? Troy asked. "This young fella is my son, Fraser. He is ten years old and can't wait to go fishing," announced Del. "Well your dad certainly brought you to the right place, Fraser. I'm sure you will catch lots of fish," commented Troy. "Thank-you Mr.," squeaked Fraser, blushing. "Here is your room key. Number 22. We hope you two enjoy your stay. If there is anything we can do to to make your visit here more pleasurable, please let us know," stated Traci. "Thanks very much, and call me Del," he replied as the father and son left.

Early the next morning Del and Fraser stopped and had breakfast at Dunkin Donuts followed by a trip to Lavron Lure's. They had the basics when it came to fishing gear, but they needed bait and maybe a couple of lures. When the two pushed through the big red door, ringing the bell on top, it was like going back in time. The creaky floors and narrow isles gave character to the place. The aroma of freshly brewed coffee lingered in the air. As they took their time looking at different fishing equipment, Buzz asked if there is anything he could help with. "We just came in for some worms, but could you point out some lures that are effective?" Del queried. "For sure I can. Come with me." Buzz stated as they ambled over three isles. "Down this row you will find all kinds of lures. They are all effective depending on what you are fishing for.

These red and green spinners will trick many fish," explained Buzz. "That is terrific mister, thanks. We'll take a couple different spinners then," announced Del.

"You don't look familiar. Are you from around these parts?" questioned Buzz. "No sir. My son and I are here to participate in your derby. We got here yesterday and are staying at the Ozark Inn," remarked Del. "Welcome to our town mister. I certainly hope you enjoy your stay. I know the owners of the Inn. They are nice folks," admitted Buzz. "Yes they are. By the way, the last time I was here, there was a big controversy about a large car parts company moving to Lavron. What became of that?" Del inquired. "Well that parts company got their way. The massive plant is almost complete. In order to get their way, they also built a Movie Theatre and Community Center for our town to enjoy," replied Buzz. "Well I hope everything works in favor for your Municipality." Del added. "That remains to be seen, but as long as they keep to themselves, I don't see any harm," uttered Buzz.

Del and Fraser shopped around a little more, grabbed some bait, paid the dues for the Derby and departed. Fraser could not wait one more day for the tournament to begin. The two drove to Lake of the Ozark's to pick out a couple of desirable spots to drop in a line. They stopped by the Bagnell dam just to see the sheer size of it. It was something to see. With its eight huge generators, the dam serves purpose. "Before the 1930's, all this water was land. They built this dam to produce electricity, but it also produced a massive lake." Del informed his son. "Wow! And now we get to fish in it," replied Fraser. The Phillips's tentatively picked out a few spots to fish, then headed back to the Motel.

Friday morning couldn't come fast enough. Fraser was up at the crack of dawn. After getting dressed, loading up the car and stopping for breakfast, the father and son drove to a part of the lake they thought would be fruitful. They were not alone. "Holy smokes, look at all of these people out here already dad." Fraser observed. "I knew this was a popular derby, buy holy smokes is right son." Del mentioned gawking around. Del drove a little further to where it was less populated and parked his car. "This area is as good as any other, I suppose. Let's give it a try Fraser," stated Del. Del made sure that his son was set up properly to cast that first line. "Away you go bud, good luck." "Thanks dad," remarked Fraser with a smile from ear to ear. When the young lad reeled in his first Trout, dad had the camera ready. The fish weighed only about a pound, not worth keeping, but the memory would last for a lifetime. A fishing derby is where a father and son can bond, apparently. They fished in that spot all morning. Most of the fish they caught were too small but the fun was exceptional. The smile on Fraser's face lasted all morning.

When Del and Fraser ran out of worms. Del hooked up the red and green spinner that Buzz sold him and three casts in, something big hit his line. Del struggled fighting and reeling the fish in. "Grab the fishing net son. This baby isn't getting away!" yelled Del. Fraser sprinted to the back seat of the car, got the net and ran it to his dad, so that he could scoop the fish into the net. Del's rod was bent almost in half. The fish was putting up a campaign to stay in the lake but Del had other ideas. Ten minutes later Fraser and dad worked together to scoop the fish into the net. When Del brought the fish out of the water, they had no idea what species it could be. It weighed approximately ten pounds and was still fighting to get back in the water. "I have never seen a fish that looks like that son. It is one ugly fish. Let's go and get it weighed. I bet Buzz knows what species it is," declared Del. "Okay dad. I'm getting hungry anyways." replied Fraser.

The guys loaded the car and drove to Lavron Lure's. When they arrived, Buzz was standing by his scale weighing another angler's catch. Del pulled the fish out of the trunk and strolled with his son, the twenty feet to where Buzz was stationed. "Well, looks like this young fellow caught himself a sure winner," announced Buzz. "That spinner you sold us, was responsible for catching this fish. The thing is, we have no idea what kind of fish it is," stated Del. "That fish is what they call a Lake Sturgeon. They are rarely caught as the population of some fish are dwindling." Buzz mentioned.

Buzz helped Del hook the Sturgeon to the scale. Fraser and dad were thrilled to see that the fish weighed 11.2 pounds. The father and son team had Buzz take a picture of the two of them, one each side of the large fish. "I doubt anyone else will bring a Lake Sturgeon in this weekend gentlemen. You may just have won yourself a canoe,"offered Buzz. "That is awesome!" Fraser blurted jumping up and down. That big smile had not gone away. "The thing is mister, we are leaving tomorrow. I have to get back," replied Del. "Not to worry. If you do win, you can take the prize or the equivalent in cash." Buzz offered. "That is terrific!" remarked Del. "I can have this fish cleaned, and if you want, Hungry Hank's will either smoke it or deep fry it for you. They are quite tasty," stated Buzz. "That is a great idea. I can't believe how hospitable everyone is, here in Lavron. Thank-you Buzz." Del postulated. "Not a problem guys. I will call ahead to the restaurant. Come back in an hour or so and your Sturgeon will be ready. It will certainly be, all you can eat," laughed Buzz.

That evening Del and Fraser were somewhat celebrities. The staff at Hungry Hank's brought out the Sturgeon on two plates, nicely dressed with red potatoes and mushy peas. "Here you are gents. We hope you enjoy your dinner. We don't see too many Sturgeon here anymore. They seem to be disappearing."

The server placed the two plates on the table. "Thank-you very much. Why are the Sturgeon disappearing?" inquired Del. "I'm not too sure actually. I've heard different reports of some species dying out. My guess is the lake is getting polluted." Stated the young women. "Well we do not need that, do we?" insisted Del. "No we don't," and the server left.

Del relished his dinner. He had never eaten Sturgeon before. Fraser struggled with his, but put on a brave face and ate most of his dinner. "You know buddy; we are like pioneers. We are eating what we caught today. How would you like to live like that all of the time?" "It was fun dad, but getting food at the grocery store is a little more convenient," added Fraser with another smile. "When we get home, I want you to show mom the picture, and tell her that you caught that fish. She will be so proud of you, as I am son," reflected Del.

Buzz's derby went off without a hitch, other than a few complaints about overcrowding. The three-day event brought in plenty of business for Lavron Lure's and kept everyone chatting and gossiping about who caught what, and how big. The derby got the residents and the visitors jointly connected for the same reason. If there was any animosity between the two, it was gone for three days. Fraser unfortunately did not win first prize. Another angler from out of town won first with a 14-pound Brown Trout. Buzz figured that the young lad would be happy with a new rod and reel for coming in second place. *He will be surprised when he receives them by courier,* Buzz thought. Third spot went to none other than Brock Duchin for bringing in an 8.4-pound Pike.

Chapter 13

All the dignitaries were gathered in front of the newly completed structure on Draper Street. The massive building was painted sky blue and stood out as the largest plant in the area. Grayson Manufacturing's CEO, CFO and the rest of their Board, as well as Mayor Taylor and most of the town's Council were on hand for the ribbon cutting ceremony. Buck Fendley was there with his camera to document the event, along with a few dozen citizens. It seemed as if everyone wanted to tour the building, but that would come afterwards. "Today is an historic day in Lavron. We would like to officially welcome Grayson Manufacturing International to our town. This has been mega project that has taken two and a half years of planning and building. Today we stand in front of the finest, modern, State-of-the-art facilities.

With the help of Grayson's Chief Executive Officer, Mike Hayes, we would like to cut this ribbon and wish Grayson Manufacturing a long, profitable and safe operation," exclaimed Taylor. The Mayor then took a step back, allowing Hayes speak. "This certainly has been an exhausting and herculean project, right from the get-go. We would like to thank Fox Construction for the great work they did and in a timely fashion. We also would like to thank Lavron's Council for allowing us to move forward in our strategic approach to evolve the business. Grayson is thrilled to call Lavron home and we will be forever grateful," declared Hayes. And with that the two men sliced the yellow ribbon. There was a round of applause as everyone waited to be taken on the Grand tour.

The tour, headed by Fox Construction's Foreman Pete Hawkins, began in the front offices. The offices were current and contemporary with ergonomic seating and computer screens that could raise and lower for the user's comfort. "Now as we enter the production area, I will remind you all, please do not to touch anything and remain with the group," stated Pete. For the most part, no one really knew what they were looking at, until Pete explained exactly what that particular machines function was for. There were casting, molding and milling machines that produced different automotive parts. The automation was incredible! "Most of the pieces would be manufactured in record time, with pinpoint accuracy. The equipment here can get very loud and very warm.

These machines are cooled with a water and oil blend. You will notice the safety features around each piece of machinery. Safety is key here at Grayson." Pete admitted.

One of the people taking the tour raised their hand. "We have a question, yes ma'am," asked Hawkins. "You mentioned that the machines are cooled with a water and oil blend. How do you dispose of that concoction?" asked Laura Rush. "That mixture will be recycled to the point that it won't be useful any longer, then we will pump it into fifty gallon drums and ship it to a disposal company. Some of the mixture will be separated, filtered, tested and reclaimed," explained Pete. Laura seemed happy with Pete's explanation. Jim Lambert was trying to stay inconspicuous, hiding in the middle of the group. He decided to stay back as everyone moved on with the tour.

Hawkins brought the assembly into the five story Warehouse. There seemed to be endless rows of yellow racking. "This is where the parts will be stored for distribution across America. Before long this whole facility will be full. We have seventeen docks that will be in constant use. Raw materials coming in, and finished products going out," announced Hawkins. "There will be twenty forklift trucks working around the clock to make things run efficiently." Pete continued. The group followed Pete through the huge warehouse as he pointed out more safety features. Fire extinguishers and eye wash stations were littered all around the building.

There were Stop signs at every intersection with a warning to sound your horn. "Next Monday, is when we get the ball rolling. It will take a week to get production flowing, and then it will be full steam ahead. We expect to be able to complete intricate orders on a daily basis, exclaimed Hawkins.

Jim climbed a dozen stairs to where a milling machine was located. He discovered exactly where it was that the liquid blend cooled the machine. Underneath the apparatus was a drain leading to another device, labeled, "Chiller". This obviously is where the mixture would be cooled and recycled. From there the liquid is pumped through the machine again, but this time the used blend goes to a different drain. Jim took note of this, but then hurried back to the tour without being noticed.

The tour ended as it began, through the offices. Everyone was impressed. The members of Town Council that went on the tour, were happy that they made the right decision. Buck Fendley took lots of pictures that would be displayed throughout the Herald in the next edition. The group thanked Pete for the Grand tour then slowly dispersed to their vehicles.

Grayson was the talk of the town for the next few days. Residents would drive by just to have a glimpse of the mega plant. Lavron had a Movie Theatre and Community Center now. Most of the citizen's viewed this as a fair trade. Some of the people couldn't understand what all the fuss was about in the beginning.

Lavron continued to be the humble, bustling little town it always was. Vacationer's visiting Lavron, would enjoy the pleasant, relaxing atmosphere that the citizens provided. The scenery was second to none. One hiker that got lost for a day, explained that, although he didn't know where he was, he was not worried. "You can easily live off of the land," he declared after being located. That statement was in an article published in the Herald, along with pictures and a full story of his adventure.

It doesn't matter if you are an angler, hiker, bird watcher, hunter or just a visitor, you will have a story to tell afterwards. This is why Lavron has many returning travelers, and at this time of year the hunters were coming back for Duck season.

Autumn is a bittersweet season in Lavron. Although still fairly busy, the residents see a drop in the population and the temperature. Soon there will be no more visitors, and the town will go back to sleep for the winter months. Grayson on the other hand was booming. Business had never been better. The strategic move to build here had paid off. For a plant to produce record amounts of automotive parts with a skeleton crew, was truly amazing. Grayson's stock had climbed and their competitors were not liking it. The Board of Trustees were worried about industrial espionage.

The new plant had decent security with cameras around the perimeter, and swipe cards for employee entry, but they had decided to beef up the security. With that, there was be a gate installed in the front of the building, and warnings about "No" pictures allowed to be taken on the premises. The truck drivers were to stay in their vehicles and would be told when they have been loaded or off loaded. Any visitors to the Site were asked a series a security questions before being taken directly to where they need to be.

Chapter 14

Megan Fournier graduated with Honors in Aquatic Botany from Lincoln University. She still works part time for the Tourist Information Center but had locked down a position with an Environmental Geoscience company and had been given a small laboratory to work out of, right in Lavron. She is responsible for taking samples of soil, water, bedrock and different ecosystems throughout the Ozark Plain. She would make reports of any changes in this area, no matter how small. This is right up Megan's alley. There had been some concern about unwanted build ups of algae in Lake of the Ozark's. This had been happening slowly but, each year it became more evident. A lake this size does not freeze completely in winter, and Megan could still get the samples she needs for the Lab.

She was concerned that, if this was not taken care of quickly, an environmental disaster was not far away. This much algae growth is not natural and Megan suspects that an unscrupulous company was polluting the lake. Fertilizer causes algae growth and she had investigated that issue. But, she had found no such company producing fertilizer. This was not her only concern. Other pollutants had been discovered as well. In some parts of the lake, patches of oil had been found floating. The rainbow colored greasy sludge is definitely a threat to the environment. Megan has sent many reports to her Supervisor advising an in depth investigation. Missouri Geoscience had reassured her that an investigation would happen in the Spring when further analysis could be examined. They had given Megan other projects to focus on for the time being.

Winter in Lavron was different this year. The residents had other options. Instead of staying inside and watching television or reading etc., citizens could go for a swim, go to a movie or get some exercise in the gym/ Basketball court.

The talk around town was about Grayson's generosity and how everyone had been enjoying the new facilities. Other than seeing more Transport trucks coming and going through town, no one has noticed any interference or disruption from the mega manufacturing plant. Lavron's Council had made the right choice.

Greg and Brock had been asked to help with flooding, from an off shoot of the Osage river. They had some experience with explosives and needed to unblock a buildup of ice, that was backing up the river. Anyone dealing with dynamite had to have proper qualifications. Thanks to St. Louis University, both Greg and Brock had their diploma's in demolition. Safety and security were top priority when it comes to explosives. It was predetermined that only the amount of dynamite needed would be authorized. In this particular case, eighteen individual pieces of TNT would be needed, and placed in strategic areas around the blockage. The brothers drove to the flooded region and realized that this was a bigger job that they first though. The flood waters were threatening some farmland, and if not taken care of immediately, next year's crops could be at risk. Greg and Brock, wearing the proper protection, knew exactly where to place the dynamite. Greg drilled holes in the ice and Brock slid the mini bombs into the cavity. It was time consuming but they manage to have most of the TNT in the proper location by noon. "I have a feeling that someone miscalculated the amount of dynamite we need. We have eleven sticks in the right positions and no more are to be allocated," mentioned Greg. "I won't tell if you won't, big brother." Brock stated with a smile. "Mum's the word then buddy," declared Greg.

The guys broke for lunch, hoping that when they detonated the TNT, the blast will clear the blockage of ice thats was causing all the anguish. Once the brothers finished their bagged lunch, they double checked that all connections were flawless and the wiring exact. They then put on their ear protection. "Well, are you ready for some fireworks Greg," yelled Brock with his finger on the trigger. "Let 'er go buddy," Greg insisted. The explosion was spectacular. Eleven sticks of dynamite going off simultaneously caused instant chaos. Huge chunks of ice flew in all directions opening up the river once again. The water started to flow nicely, taking the water from the fields with it. In a matter of a couple hours the fields would return to normal for this time of year. After inspecting their handy work and being satisfied with the outcome, the brothers packed up all their equipment and headed back to the Yard, minus seven sticks of TNT.

Blooms Flower Shop was immersed with activity. Valentine's day was just around the corner and Trish Burns was up for the challenge. Orders were coming in consistently. It seems that Lavron is no different from any other small town.

Love was in the air and not long from now, so would be Spring. Troy stopped in to get Traci a bouquet of roses and was surprised to see Jim Lambert hovering over some different arrangements. "Whats happening Jimmy?" asked Troy. "Hi Troy. Not much going on. Just getting something for the wife. I suppose you are doing the same, eh?" replied Jim. "That would be correct Jim. Hey, I didn't get a chance to take the tour of the Grayson plant, but I did read the write up about it in the paper. It looked pretty interesting," remarked Troy. "Yes, it certainly was interesting to the point of culpability. I still have my suspicions about Grayson, and only time will tell. During the tour I was able to get away from the group for a few minutes and saw how they cooled the machines. I'm almost positive that liquid is only recycled once and then disposed of through a drain in the floor," voiced Jim. "Did you ask any questions about what you suspect, Jimmy?" Troy wondered with concern. "I couldn't because we were all supposed to be stick together in the group. They probably thought that I went to the washroom," answered Jim. "We do not need an enigma troubling our town. If this proves to be true, I will call another meeting with our little group. I'm sure Buzz would welcome us in his storage room again," declared Troy. "Right you are my friend. We will keep a close eye on the situation, Troy. Now I had better get something for the missus and get out of here," admitted Jim. The two shook hands and parted.

Valentine's day was a busy day for many of businesses. The restaurants and bars were to capacity and the theatre was packed with couples celebrating the day. The shelves of any store that sold chocolate and other candy were empty. Trish kept up with all the flower orders and noticed that her inventory had been depleted. *"Another successful Valentine's day,"* Trish thought as she swept the floor. The next big day for her shop would be Easter, but there were always birthdays and of course, funerals.

The first signs of Spring come in early March. Any snow that was lingering is now dissipated and the temperatures are starting to warm. There was always the chance of one more freak snow storm, but the residents of Lavron felt that the bulk of winter is behind them and it was time to get out of the house and into the yard. Gardens needed to be cleaned up and toiled and lawns needed to be raked. It seemed like everyone lived for this time of year. With only a month to prepare, Buzz was busy ordering supplies for his shop. He knows from years gone by, that he had better over stock his inventory as April proves to be the busiest. Buzz's storage room will be full with anything you may need regarding fishing, hunting or hiking. As a goodwill gesture, Buzz made sure that the hiker that got lost for a day out exploring, received a compass, courtesy of Lavron Lure's.

The bell at the top of the door entering the store rang. Greg and Brock stormed in looking overly concerned. "Good morning men. Whats going on?" questioned Buzz. "Buzz, we were sent out to clean up the shoreline around the lake. You will not believe the absolute mess out there," cried Brock. "What are you talking about guys? Surly the ice has gone," inquired Buzz. Greg stepped forward. "Listen Buzz, we have never witnessed what we saw today. There are algae all over the shore, along with dead fish and patches of oil floating along the shoreline," admitted Greg being animated. "What the hell are you talking about.? Oil and dead fish. No way guys. Maybe someone lost a tank of gas from their boat, but, come on, that has to be a fluke," remarked Buzz. "It's more than that Buzz. We walked about a mile up the east shore. Not all of it is ruined, but a good part of it is. We wanted to let you to know before we go to the authorities," announced Greg. "If it is as bad as you say, by all means report it, but I would get Megan Fournier involved. She knows what to do, and who to advise," retorted Buzz. "Good idea. We will see if she is at the Tourism outlet. Thanks Buzz," replied Greg as the two men left the shop.

Buzz started worrying. What the hell happened to the lake to cause such devastation? The twins must be exaggerating. Algae, oil, dead fish. Maybe in a small portion of the water, but not what they are describing. Buzz decided to take a drive out to the lake after work and see for himself.

When Greg and Brock pulled into the parking lot of the Tourist Information Center in the Town's pick-up truck, there was just one other vehicle in the driveway. Luckily it was Megan's Jeep. The two guys stepped into the small log cabin and spotted Megan stapling a trail map to the wall.

"Hi Meg. How are you?" the guys said simultaneously. "Well if it isn't the Duchin brothers. What brings you two in here?" questioned Megan with a wide smirk. "Honestly Megan, it's not good news. We were at the lake this morning. Something is terribly wrong. For at least a mile along the east shoreline, the is a ton of algae, oil and dead fish. Buzz mentioned that you would know what to do and who to inform," remarked Greg. "I have sent in many reports proving that the lake is getting polluted. My supervisor tells me that an investigation will take place in May." Megan reflected. "May! It will be too late by May!" pronounced Brock with his voice elevated. "Something needs to be done now before Buzz's fishing derby," remarked Greg. "I understand boys, but let me tell you something. This is the government we are talking about. Nothing gets done quickly when it comes to the government figuring things out," replied Megan. "I have a feeling that they would pick up the pace, if we showed them a few pictures of the utter desolation we witnessed this morning Megan," admitted Greg. "That is a great idea Greg. Go back and take lots of photos. I will e-mail them directly to my boss and see if that wakes him up," explained Meg. "Bingo! Come on Brock, let's get some pics for the young lady," stated Greg winking at Megan.

Chapter 15

It didn't take long for the news to get around town and to Missouri Geoscience. Megan's supervisor, Joe Hamilton, immediately forwarded the information to Herb Turner's office. The Environmental Minister could not believe what had taken place and quickly sent out a team to investigate the infected area of Lake of the Ozark's. Herb himself, wanted to get a first-hand look at the devastation. He and Joe Hamilton agreed to meet the following day at the east part of the lake where all the evidence shows. Joe asked Megan to be present and to bring her files from the last three years. The investigating team would already have gotten a full day's work in by then, and hopefully some clue as to what had happened.

Herb, Joe and Meg met at 10 am. on the east shore of the lake. There were greetings all round before they decided to take a walk up the coast. "You have been studying the lake for some time Megan. When was it that you discovered the increase in algae growth?" queried Herb.

"Well sir, the truth is, most of my studies are of a personal nature. I noticed an increase in algae growth three years ago, but nothing serious. I grew up here and always loved this lake. It is only in the last year that the Ministry started keeping records. And none too soon, as you can see," admitted Meg.

"Algae does not cause fish to die. As you know it can happen naturally," reflected Joe. "I'm afraid that algae is not the culprit here. That floating rainbow over there is," insisted Herb pointing to a twenty-foot-wide circle of oil. "Right you are Mr. Turner," replied Joe. "We will have to wait and see what the investigation team comes up with. If there is oil all through the lake, we will find the guilty party and prosecute to the full extent of the law," promised the Minister. The three strolled up the shoreline and could not believe the mess. Algae, seaweed and dead fish littered the shore. "This is truly a manmade disaster. The lake was fine this time last year," mentioned Megan. "And other than an increase in algae, you have not noticed any pollution, Miss Fournier?" asked Herb. "I suspected that the increase in algae was due to someone discarding fertilizer into the lake but I have not confirmed that as of yet. As for the oil, I had only heard rumors," voiced Meg. "So a year ago we had absolutely no issue with pollutants?" questioned Joe. "None of any significance," suggested Meg. Herb Turner then remembered that the only new factory in the area was Grayson Manufacturing.

Herb then decided to get his investigative team to focus on Grayson. For the last year they have been sending water samples to the Ministry for analyzing and every sample had been within regulations. The Environmental Minister knew that there are ways to "fix" the waste water to be within the regulations, but after the trouble Grayson has been in, in the past, they surely would clean up their act. "I will get the team to map out how much oil is out there. Hopefully we can stop the damage now and get this entire mess cleaned up quickly," pronounced the Minister. "That sounds encouraging sir," said Megan.

Herb thought of an attack plan. He would gather another team of experts along with the police to storm Grayson's premises and try to find incriminating evidence that yes, it is them polluting the lake. "I want to thank you Joe and Megan for coming here today. I think now, I have a good idea as to who is doing this to the lake," noted Herb. Joe and Meg looked at each other wishing they knew what Herb knew. "It was our pleasure to meet you, sir. We just wish it was under different circumstances," replied Joe.

The three of them walked back to their vehicles and shook hands. "My office will keep you posted as to what transpires. Thank-you again for accompanying me. It was my pleasure as well." Herb retorted.

Herb drove back to his office and immediately called a meeting with the investigative team and the authorities. They would have to figure out a plan to surprise Grayson Manufacturing's site. It would have to be quick and precise, to the point that no employee would have a chance to alter or switch any procedure that they have in place. It would be a raid. Jefferson City's Chief of Police, George Reid, suggested a full Swat team storm the premises and let the Environmental authorities investigate. Not only will they test all the machinery for contaminants but the cooling mixture as well. They will also need documentation on how much waste is produced and what disposal company excepts it and when.

When the committee finalized their plan, they would get everything in place for two days from now.

The raid would take place at a time when no one could expect such an event, 6 am.

When Megan got back to her lab, she called Greg. She liked the wink she got from Greg back at the Tourist Center. "Hi Greg. Listen, I was just with the Minister of the Environment. You were absolutely right. Someone or something is polluting the lake," stressed Meg. "I kind of figured that darlin'. Brock and I discovered something suspicious behind Grayson's plant. It's like a shaft or tunnel leading from the plant to the river. We looked into it, but were convinced that nothing bad would transpire. I guess we could be wrong Meg," admitted Greg. "Thanks for that information Greg. I will let my boss know. He will tell the proper authorities. I have a feeling something big is going to happen," exclaimed Meg. "I really hope that Grayson is the guilty party here. We have had a bad taste in our mouth ever since they started talks with the Town," insisted Greg. "Would you mind taking me to where this shaft is Greg? I would like to see it first hand," asked Megan. "Not a problem girl. How about after work today?" questioned Greg. "That would be great." "Ok then. Can I pick you up just after four?" urged Greg. "That would be fine. I will look forward to it Mr. Duchin." Meg replied. "Not more than I Ms. Fournier," joked Greg. The two ended their conversation but couldn't wait to see each other later in the afternoon.

Megan knew that she had better change her clothes if she was going into the bush. At noon she drove home and got into some khaki pants and a loose fitting top. She put on a little perfume as well. Greg arrived at the Tourist Center shortly after 4 and was surprised that Megan was waiting on the steps looking terrific. "Hop in good looking," proposed Greg with a wide smile. "Well thank-you Gregory. I brought my camera with me to capture any evidence that could incriminate Grayson," confessed Meg. "Great idea girl. I'm hoping that the passageway by the plant is still evident. It certainly was a year ago. I'm hoping that it hasn't grown over with shrubs and grass," explained Greg. "How exactly do we get to this spot?" asked Meg. "Brock and I trampled a path to behind the plant. The river is only about sixty feet away and is flowing rapidly at that point. Not to get off of the subject Meg, but there is some good fishing there as well," revealed Greg.

Greg parked his Corolla behind another factory. The two got out of the car and proceeded to the manmade path. At this time of year, the new growth hindered their route but they trudged on. Twenty minutes later, they appeared to be where Brock found the tunnel from the plant to the river. It had grown over but Greg hunted around until he discovered what were definitely track marks from a tractor. "You see here Meg that there are grader tracks right from the building to the river," stated Greg. Megan started trampling the tall grass down. "You are absolutely right Greg." Meg observed as she clicked a few photos.

At that point as harsh voice came from about forty feet away. "You two, what are you doing here, this is private property," yelled a large man wearing a navy blue uniform with yellow badges on the arms and chest. He had what resembled a shotgun. "The young lady and I are out looking for a good fishing spot," lied Greg. "I don't see how you need a camera to look for a fishing spot, now get out of here before I get mad," shouted the Guard. That sparked a nerve in Greg. He doesn't get angry often, but this guy was pushing his buttons. "This is Government land not private property." Greg declared as he started walking towards the man. "My little shotgun here says that this is Grayson's property and unless you want to taste some lead, I suggest you bugger off," asserted the Guard. "I hope you realize that you probably just incriminated the company you piece of shit," stated Megan. Just then the guy raised the shotgun into the air and fired a shot. It was loud and it echoed throughout the bush. Greg grabbed Megan's hand and they quickly exited the area, but not before Meg got a picture of the Guard.

Megan did not let go of Greg's hand. He guided her back through the bush and to his car. She was obviously shaken by the incident. "It's okay Meg. At least we know now that Grayson is trying to hide or cover something up," mentioned Greg as he hugged Megan to calm her down. "I have got to get back, and let Joe Hamilton know what has happened. This is bigger than we first though. Grayson is guilty of polluting the lake. There is no question in my mind about that Greg," asserted Meg.

The ride back to the Center was quiet. Megan seemed to mellow from the shock of a shotgun going off. Greg stopped his car beside hers at the Center. "Thanks for the excitement Greg," she offered. "I'm sorry about that Meg. I certainly didn't think anything like that would happen," admitted Greg. "Maybe you could make it up to me with a drink at the Piper tonight?" lured Megan. "It's a date. And don't you change your mind. I will pick you up at 8," announced Greg. "See you then," replied Megan as she gave him a peck on his cheek.

Megan got into her Jeep and drove to her lab. She had to let Joe know immediately about what had transpired. She did not e-mail him but called him directly. His phone rang four times before he answered. "Mr. Hamilton, it's Megan," she uttered franticly. "Something is very wrong at the Grayson plant. A friend took me to the back of Grayson Manufacturing's property and it looks like an underground shaft or tunnel has been inserted. It goes from the plant, right to the Osage river that is only about sixty feet away. When we were there, some kind of Security Guard threatened us with a shotgun and told us to leave. When we resisted somewhat, he raises the gun in the air and fired a shot," rambled Meg. "Calm down Miss Fournier. Are you absolutely sure this guy belonged to Grayson?" retorted Joe. "He was wearing a Security Guard uniform and was standing on Grayson's property sir," replied Megan. "Are you okay? Was anyone hurt in the altercation?" asked Joe. "Both my friend and I are fine, just shaken up. I haven't been threatened with a shotgun before," stated Meg. "You did the right thing, calling me straight away Megan. Leave it with me now. Action will be taken a.s.a.p. but please stay away from the plant. It sounds like you have been through enough for one day," insisted Joe. "No worries there sir. You won't see me anywhere near Grayson's plant for a long time," responded Meg. "Good to hear Megan. Now, I want you to make a full report about what happened and e-mail it to me. And I also want you to take tomorrow off. Is that understood?" urged Joe. "Yes Mr. Hamilton, understood," answered Meg.

Joe wasted no time contacting the Ministry of the Environment. Herb himself was in another meeting and shouldn't be disturbed. Joe explained to Herb's secretary that this information was paramount and to barge in and get him out of the meeting. She was very reluctant, but after Joe practically screamed at her, she decided that maybe this guy had some important news. She asked Joe to hang on and she would do what she could. Through the intercom she told Herb that she had a frantic guy on the phone with important information that he needs to hear. He excused himself and took the call in another office. "Herb Turner speaking," he said aggressively. "Mr. Turner, it's Joe Hamilton. Megan Fournier and a friend if hers went to the back of Grayson Manufacturing's property and were threatened with a shotgun and told to get off the land, but not before they discovered tractor marks going from the plant to the Osage river. They believe that there is a buried shaft or tunnel beneath those tracks," exclaimed Joe. "Is everyone alright? No one got hurt?" questioned Herb. "Everyone is fine, they are just shaken up, but this tells us that Grayson is not playing fair," insisted Joe. "Joe, I can't tell you what we are planning, but something big is going down and very soon. Thank-you for the call. And please tell Megan and her friend to stay far away from the Grayson's site," demanded Herb. "I don't think you will need to worry about that sir. They had enough excitement for one day," replied Joe.

As promised, Greg picked Megan up at 8. She looked beautiful with straightened hair and a short skirt. It was a big change from khaki pants and an oversized top. She came to his car with a wide smile. "Long time, no see," stated Meg. "Too long Megan. I missed you," retorted Greg returning the smile. The two young individuals had lots in common as they discovered on their date. Greg was a perfect gentleman and Megan flirted enough to keep him on his toes. When they left the Piper, they were holding hands, and when Greg dropped her off at home, Greg got more than a peck on the cheek. "I had a great time Meg. Can we do this again real soon?" pleaded Greg. "I would like that very much Mr. Duchin." replied Meg. After another round of kisses, Megan bid Greg, bye for now with promises of see him in the very near future.

Chapter 16

Greg had developed feelings for Megan and couldn't wait to see her again, but he knew that Grayson was definitely guilty. It all added up. Patches of oil on the lake along with dead fish, and a security guard threatening an innocent couple with a shotgun. Greg got hold of his brother and told him what had happened. They both knew that Buzz's derby was in three weeks and decided to let him in on the news. At noon the next day they went to see Buzz at his store. "Buzz, we are afraid that your derby may be in trouble. What we saw on the lake is disturbing but according to Megan Fournier it is even worse than we thought. The Ministry was here yesterday and they have narrowed this mess back to Grayson. Believe it or not Buzz, Meg and I were threatened with a shotgun yesterday afternoon by a security guard at the back of Grayson's property," exclaimed Greg. "Well boys, we all had an idea that Grayson was crooked. Now it's time for us to do something about it," replied Buzz. Brock suddenly got quiet and whispered; "We happen to have seven sticks of TNT at our disposal Buzz." "Now we're talking guys. Maybe a clandestine meeting tonight at the back of the property is in order?" Buzz queried. "That sounds like a good idea Buzz but, Megan believes that Herb Turner is planning some kind of action against

Grayson, and soon!" admitted Greg. "Okay. That is even better guys. Let them deal with Grayson, and we will deal with them afterwards, if you know what I mean?" Buzz said with an evil look. The three men decided to keep one another posted as to what happens. Brock will go and get the dynamite that he hid earlier. They also thought it would be best to keep this between the three of them. It was not necessary to let the rest of their group in on it, although they would willingly volunteer.

The SWAT team from Jefferson City rolled into Lavron at 4 am. They were disguised in Ford vans with signs that advertised Commercial and Residential painting. The ladders on top added to the camouflage. The vans stopped before Draper Street. The crew went over their plan with the blueprints in front of them. Four groups of four men will surround the building. At this time of day, they are betting that no one is watching the security cameras. At precisely 6 am with synchronized timing, the four groups will break down the doors and rush to exact locations in the building.

One group will go straight to the main office. They don't expect that many personnel will be there but, they will be in charge of this shift and the team wants to shut down any communication, whether it be cell phone or intercom. The next group will go to the cooling systems to determine what the ratio of oil to water is in the mixture, and how it is recycled, if indeed it is at all. The third group will have already rounded up Grayson's security people and the fourth group will make sure no one leaves the premises. The Commander gave to code word at exactly 6 am. The raid took less than twenty minutes. All the thirty-five employees were in shock. They could not believe what was happening. They were told that until further notice Grayson Manufacturing International is shut down. No one will be arrested at this time and the CEO has been notified. The Ministry of the Environment will determine if there has been any wrong doing here.

Mike Hayes was out of his mind with anger. "What the hell are you talking about?" Mike yelled into the phone. It was six in the morning. "I have just explained Mr. Hayes that your facility has been raided for reasons we feel necessary for the safety of the environment." Herb Turner's secretary vocalized. "You better have a well-documented reason for doing so, miss. I am on my way," blurted Hayes. "We will be waiting for you, sir. Drive carefully," she said with a smirk.

Mike wasted no time calling his CFO, Bill Landry. In a matter of minutes, the pair were flying down highway 54 towards Lavron. "You know as well as I do Mike that the concentration of coolant cannot exceed an 85 to 15 ratio," stated Bill. "Yes, I do know that, and that is how it was to be set in the system. No one would be able to detect any toxins if that were the case. Something went wrong if they raided the plant," admitted Mike. "I only hope the technician operating the cooling system was able to switch the recycling line back to the plant and not to the river," suggested Bill. "That my friend is our only hope," replied Mike.

The rest of the drive was pretty quiet. Both executives knew that jail time would await them if the Ministry determines Grayson has indeed polluted Lake of the Ozark's. When Mike and Bill pull up to the site, yellow tape had been placed around the mega plant warning to stay clear of the area. The building had been secured except for a couple of doors that had been broken down.

The first thing Mike did when he got out of his car was ask who was in charge of this fiasco and where is the Search Warrant? The Commander of the raid introduced himself as Bob Askins and handed the Warrant to Mike. When Mike and Bill found the paperwork in order, the next thing was to plead innocent. "We have no idea what you people want from us. What is it you are looking for?" asked Bill. "We will let the Ministry answer that for you, sir. They are in the building now searching for evidence that Grayson is polluting the waterways," replied Bob. "That is ridiculous, Grayson is, and has always been a reputable company. We know that the environment, especially in this region is key to everyone's wellbeing," lied Mike. "Right you are sir. I'm sure the Ministry will be here for quite a while. You are not allowed in the building so, I suggest the two of you go get a coffee and relax. They will let you know what transpires," advised Bob.

As always, news travels fast around Lavron. When Jim Lambert got wind of what was happening, he and Buck Fendley raced to Draper Street to find emergency vehicles blocking Grayson Manufacturing's entrance. They couldn't get closer than fifty feet of the massive building. Buck took pictures of the barricaded plant that would make the front page of the Herald. Jim tried to interview Bob Askins but he was tight lipped about the event. He recognized Mike Hayes sitting in his car sipping coffee. Mike was all too happy to give his side of the story. He stressed that Lavron had a conspiracy against Grayson right from the beginning. If anything was discovered in the building that would incriminate Grayson, it was planted! Mike reassured the town that if someone was polluting the lake, it was another entity and not them.

The investigating team concentrated on the cooling system. They found the liquid concoction that cooled the milling and molding machines. After being used, it was put through a chiller to re-cool the mixture. The team knew that this procedure could only be done so many times, before the liquid had to be changed. It wasn't until one of the team members moved a couple of fifty gallon barrels, that a secondary drain was discovered in the floor. But where did this drain lead to? The Ministry has all the latest tech equipment from x-ray hardware to heat and metal detection. It would only be a matter of time before the team would find where the drain ran to.

Greg and Brock picked Megan up at her home after hearing about the raid. They had to let the investigating team know about the shaft leading to the river. Although Joe told Herb what took place a day earlier, it slipped his mind as other plans were in the works. By the time they reached Draper Street the road was blocked off to incoming traffic. Greg parked his Corolla off to the side of the road and the three of them got out. It was a five hundred foot walk to the nearest vehicles. They thought it was strange that two vans advertising Commercial and Residential Painting were at the forefront of all the other means of transport. When they approached the area Bob Askins came out of his van to meet them.

"I'm afraid that I will have to ask you to leave this area immediately," insisted Bob. "We have information that is critical to what is going on sir," stated Greg. "And exactly what is that information?" Bob questioned. "We have reason to believe that some kind of shaft or tunnel is running from the plant to the river. We were threatened yesterday by a Security Guard," stressed Greg. "Okay, slow down big guy. What are you talking about?" queried Bob. My brother and I were at the back of this plant quite a while ago, fishing. Brock discovered trampled down grass and grader tracks. It turns out that those tracks lead right to the plant," explained Greg. "So why did you not report that to the authorities?" interrogated Askins. "We didn't feel it was necessary. We talked to the site Foreman and he explained to us that it was more or less recycled water that goes back out to the river, answered Greg. "Okay, that make sense. What were you saying about being threatened yesterday?" quizzed Bob. Megan couldn't contain herself. "I work for Missouri Geoscience. One of my responsibilities is to test and report any changes that occur naturally or otherwise in the waterways. When Greg mentioned this shaft running underground from the plant to the river, I had to see for myself. Greg brought me to the back of the property when a Guard came out with a shotgun and told us to leave. When Greg resisted somewhat, he raised the gun in the air and fired a shot," rambled Meg.

"Thank-you very much for that information. I will see to it that the investigation team checks that out immediately." Bob reassured them. "Thanks," they said in unison as they headed back to the car. Megan slipped her hand into Greg's and the two broke out smiling. "By the way Brock, Meg and I are seeing each other.

Chapter 17

Bob Askins radioed the information to the investigation team. It would have only been a matter of time before they discovered the drain shaft, but now after finding it, and oil residue throughout the shaft, they felt they had significant evidence to charge Grayson's executives with corruption and industrial pollution. Herb Turner was notified. He wanted to be on site when Mike Hayes and Bill Landry were officially charged. He told Commander Askins to hold the pair until he arrived.

Turner felt that because they had damaging evidence against Grayson, that they should open up the other two cases and look for secret drainage shafts in those facilities. He wondered just how many hundreds of millions of dollars Grayson wasted on this state-of-the-art plant, not to be re-opened until it is either sold or destroyed.

The SWAT team stayed until the Minister arrived. He witnessed Mike and Bill being arrested with great relief. He now could have crews start cleaning the Osage river and Lake of the Ozark's. Unfortunately, he knew that it may take up to a year but, they had the culprits in custody and no more pollution would enter the waterways.

Greg, Meg and Brock figured with all the excitement around Lavron, they would take the rest of the day off of work. After all they had the helped the investigative team find the appalling evidence. Greg dropped Meg off at home to have a shower and get cleaned up for another date later that day. Then the brothers decided to let Buzz in on the news of Grayson's demise. They guys strolled into Lavron Lure's to see Buzz almost in tears. "What's up Buzz? Why are you upset bud?" asked Brock with a worried look. "Boys, in a couple of weeks my derby was to begin. I went out to the lake yesterday and saw firsthand the patches of oil and the dead fish. I couldn't or wouldn't expect anyone to fish in those conditions," explained Buzz. "We certainly understand Buzz, but we did come bearing good news. It sure looks like Grayson got busted this morning and was shut down, "smiled Greg. "That is great news but the damage has been done. We all figured that Grayson was crooked, and now we suffer because of them," said Buzz wiping his eyes.

"Lavron will definitely suffer financially because of Grayson, but only until they can clean up the lake. I'm sure with today's technology they will have the lake cleaned up this time next year," exclaimed Brock. "You mentioned that you have seven sticks of TNT. I would like to make sure that Grayson will never re-open. What are you boys up to tonight?" Greg told Buzz about Megan and their date that evening. He would have her home by eleven if they wanted to congregate afterwards.

The plan was to meet at midnight and go down the path that Greg and Brock made years ago. They would go into Grayson's property from behind. They would wear dark clothing and bring flashlights, a pry bar, and the seven sticks of dynamite. Although the plant was closed the guys figured that the security cameras would still be working. They would need to be stealthy.

Greg picked Megan up just before 7 pm. Ironically he took her to a movie at the new theatre that Grayson funded. Meg thought it was funny how much popcorn Greg could consume. She nibbled on some licorice and nestled in under his arm. The action movie they watched went by quickly, so Greg thought a cocktail would be in order. Maddie Thompson, a barmaid at the River Piper was shocked to see Greg and Megan two days in a row. "What can I get you love birds tonight," she asked with a smirk. "I will have a Gin and Tonic," replied Meg blushing. "And a cold beer for me Maddie."

"By the way Greg, I have next week's schedule posted if you want to have a look," uttered Mad. "Will do. In the meantime, I think I will just look after this young lady," insisted Greg. Now it was Maddie's turn to blush. The couple enjoyed each other's company and it seemed like a relationship had developed. When Greg took Meg home, she asked if he would like to come in. He said that he would love to, but lied to her saying that they shouldn't rush into anything. He had to settle on some hugs and kisses.

Greg picked up both his brother and Buzz. It was 11:45. Brock had all the necessary equipment in a canvas bag, TNT, wire, gloves, flashlights and pry bar. They didn't dare go onto Draper Street but parked the car on another side street. They were careful not to be seen. The brothers took Buzz to the pathway that lead to the back of Grayson's property. It was very dark. They clicked on their flashlights and stuck together along the trail. Once they arrived at their destination the first thing they looked for were the security cameras.

Fortunately for them none were facing the river. They needed to find a way of entry into the building so they slowly edged down the east, and darkest side of the plant. Brock found an exit door that the SWAT team caved in. He took his pry bar and with great strength, compromised the opening. "Good job Brock," announced Buzz. Brock then took out six sticks of TNT. He split them up. Two sticks per person. "What's the other stick for," asked Buzz. "That my friend is for the Lavron Town Hall," replied Brock. "Are you sure you want to do extensive damage to the Hall? They just restored the building from that fire," questioned Buzz. "And who do you think caused that fire Buzz?" Greg smiled. "You sons of bitches. They knew the fire was arson but never found the perps. And it was you two all along," laughed Buzz. "We were suspicious of Grayson right from the start. We knew from our playing days that the Grayson site in Philadelphia was corrupt, even though they got away with polluting the Delaware River," admitted Greg. "We were hoping that our fine Mayor and Town Council would get the hint about Grayson, but obviously they didn't. That is why we have a stick of dynamite designated just for them," insisted Brock.

The guys needed to focus on the job at hand. Each piece of dynamite was to be placed on a load bearing girder. Dynamite can be set off two ways. One way is with wires leading to a detonator, the second is by fuse and matches. Brock realized that they didn't have enough wire to hook all six sticks up to the detonator, so two sticks needed to be placed where they could light the fuses and get the hell out quickly. The men entered the building. Only emergency lighting was on, so it was still quite dark. With flashlights in hand they decided to go in different directions but to meet back at the doorway in ten minutes. Buzz and Greg had the pieces that had wire running from them. Brock took the fused sticks. With Greg's guidance Buzz secured two sticks of TNT on a structural beam between a fire extinguisher. Greg then, being careful of the thin wire strode thirty yards to another weight bearing beam and repeated the process. Dragging the wire behind them, they met Brock at the designated meeting point.

Everything went well. All six pieces of TNT were put in place. Greg ran the wire outside and hooked it up to the detonator. Brock would have to re-enter the building and light the fuse that happened to be twenty feet short of the doorway. The men took a minute to breathe. "I will need to be fast. The fuse will burn quickly. I figure maybe forty-five seconds before boom time," explained Brock. They made sure that everything was in place before Brock went back inside. Greg was timing his feat. Thirty seconds later he was back outside of the building and demanded that they "RUN!" Without hesitation Greg pressed the trigger on the detonator.

The thunder and violent vibrations of steel twisting and blowing apart shocked Buzz to the core. The night sky turned crimson orange as metal and debris flew in all directions. Shrapnel from machinery and the structure itself rained everywhere. Buzz stopped running to witness the destruction just as a beam landed directly on him, killing him instantly. Greg and Brock could not believe their eyes. "What the fuck! Buzz!" screamed Greg. Buzz laid there still, blood trickling from his fractured skull. "What the hell are we going to do Brock?" cried Greg. "There is nothing we can do. Buzz is gone. We need to get out of here," shrieked Brock. The brothers looked at each other in the eyes and then bolted down the pathway. They made it to Greg's car before they saw Fire trucks racing to the scene. Greg started his car, put in reverse and fishtailed before he gained control, and sped away in the opposite direction.

They took the backroads out of town, making sure not to be seen. "What are we going to do Greg?" Brock said shaking his head. "Listen, poor Buzz is dead, but there is so much destruction, that it will be hard to determine if there was one or more persons involved. We need to get home without being seen and carry on as if nothing happened," explained Greg. "I don't know how we can do that! Buzz is gone Greg," bawled Brock. "Get hold of yourself bro. We need to do this, or we go to prison. It's as simple as that," admitted Greg. The twins were glad there was no traffic. They got to Greg's apartment and Brock decided to stay the night. Not that anyone would get any sleep, but he didn't want to take the chance of being spotted. They would go to work in a few hours as if nothing happened.

Chapter 18

Draper Street was sheer chaos. The fire crews stood back throwing water on what is now a smoldering, twisted mess. They wouldn't dare go into the crumbled structure as it was unstable and could collapse at any time. More Emergency Crews were called in from Jefferson City. The site Engineer, Steve Wilson was also asked to come survey the damage. After an explosion like this, anything could happen. A couple of police officers looking for evidence of foul play, walked the perimeter of the site.

When they reached the back of the property they saw what they believed was a body. They rushed over trying not to trip on all the rubble. Under a metal beam the two officers found the body of a fifty something male. They radioed to the Captain that they had found a deceased body. One thing had now been determined. This destruction was deliberately done. Lavron's voluntary Fire Chief, Dwayne Parsons made his way to the end of Grayson's property. He met up with officers only to see Buzz Wheeler laying there. "Oh my God! This can't be true! This man is Buzz Wheeler. He owns a fishing store here in town," explained Dwayne, not believing his eyes.

A meeting quickly commenced between the Emergency Services, Police and Fire Crews and Engineers. They decided that the best way to go about this investigation was to start from behind the plant and work their way forward. Cranes were needed to lift beams, and tractors to move the rubble.

The first thing on their priority list was to remove the deceased body. It took four men to shift the I-beam enough so that the Emergency crew could tend to the deceased. It would not be easy to extract the body out of the damaged area. They resolved the issue by waiting for a crane to arrive and lift the body out that way of the ruins.

Jim Lambert had been at the scene since he heard the fire call on his radio. He and his counterpart, Buck Fendley were trying to get a story. It wasn't until they got wind that a deceased body had been discovered, that the real story started to come together. Terrorism! Buck took many pictures, as Jim interviewed the emergency crews. They wanted to know what happened as well. One Firefighter with thirty years' experience had never witnessed such devastation. All Jim knew was he was a Captain with the last name, Kent. "Now that a body has been discovered, this will hit the News-stands across the country. This appears to be domestic terrorism. But you didn't hear that from me, understood?" insisted Kent.

Everyone turned to see a huge crane move slowly towards the devastation. The driver and operator of the crane was instructed to secure the vehicle and extend the boom so that a body could be extracted from behind the Site. Once the body had been lifted out of the zone, an ambulance was waiting to take the deceased to the morgue. Jim Lambert was beside himself when he realized that it was Buzz on that gurney. "This is just unbelievable," announced Jim to Buck who tried to get a picture. "I'm sorry Jim. I know Buzz was a good friend. It doesn't make sense," confessed Buck. Jim was stressed and confused. His mind was doing circles. He broke down in tears. *Why poor Buzz?*

A Cadillac then pulled up as close to the devastation as the police would allow. Mayor Steven Taylor emerged from the vehicle. He had security with him. When Jim spotted Mayor Turner, he quickly ran over. "Turner, this is all your fault. How dare you allow a corrupt company into Lavron!" Jim yelled as he punched him as hard as he could in the mouth, causing blood to squirt from his lips, before clutching his chest with a scream, and dropping to the ground. One security person tented to the Mayor as the other one performed CPR on Jim. The ambulance driver was called over to help. They worked on Jim for fifteen minuted before declaring him dead. Turner didn't understand why the incident occurred until he heard of Buzz's demise. He knew then, looking at the destruction, that he and Council should never have gotten involved with Grayson Manufacturing. Greg and Brock drove into work as if nothing happened. When they arrived, their boss told them about the explosions. He hadn't heard about any deaths as of yet. He suggested that they spend the day helping the emergency crews clean up any debris in and around the area, but not to interfere with the investigation. They were to report to an engineer named Steve Wilson. The guys hopped in a five-ton truck and drove to Draper Street. Looking at the destruction in daylight made it seem even more devastating. There were pipes, beams, bricks, chunks of machinery and scared racking all still smoldering or steaming. The twins saw a guy with a hard hat on and blueprints in hand. It was Wilson. Wilson advised the brothers that the Site was unstable and if they wanted to help, they could clean up the surrounding area. Apparently some guy by the name of Wheeler was responsible for this disaster and an inquiry needed to be completed in regards to his demise.

Buck was devastated. He not only lost his boss and friend, but how could the paper survive? Buck was a photographer not a columnist, but he sat down and wrote a piece as best he could about the catastrophe. The Headlines were, "Domestic Terrorism Hits Home"

The initial story was a lot of hearsay. He focused on the devastation, and why he figured it happened. Grayson had been polluting the waterways. That they knew. But for a long time, stand up resident such as Buzz Wheeler to go to such lengths to stop Grayson's activities, and to lose his life, was incredible. Was it terrorism or was it empathy for Lavron's well-being? Buzz's fishing derby was in trouble this year because of the polluted water. He took it upon himself to stop Grayson in its tracks but, unfortunately it did not turn out the way he planned. Many people will remember Buzz as a Martyr or a Hero.

Chapter 19

The investigation took many turns. It took all of eight months to finalize their inquiry. The Investigating team knew that Buzz had help before the tragedy occurred. Where did Buzz get hold of dynamite and a detonator? The team narrowed it down to the Duchin brothers, as they had been trained and worked with explosives, but that's as far as it went. There were no pieces of dynamite unspoken for, so how could they be responsible? The final outcome was that, Buzz Wheeler died as a result of not knowing the impact of so much TNT igniting in close proximity. He simply could not get out of the way quick enough.

Herb Turner was true to his word. He had clean-up crews on the lake two weeks after the devastation. He awarded Missouri Geoscience a contract to take samples from the lake and surrounding rivers and keep records of how the waterways have improved. Megan was thrilled that she now had steady employment for a long time. Greg and Brock quit their jobs with the Town and bought Lavron Lure's from Buzz's estate. The first act of business was to reinstate the fishing derby. In memory of Buzz, it would be known as "Buzz's Derby."

Lavron slowly went back to the way it was, peaceful, tranquil and serene. The tourists and anglers started coming back. Everyone that visited Lavron wanted to know where Draper Street was, so that they could drive by an empty lot that had once housed Grayson Manufacturing's State-of-the-art plant. Somehow Mayor Steven Taylor retained his job. Although Grayson was no longer a part of Lavron, the Theatre and Community Center was. That was fine with his citizens. If Turner and his Cabinet ever stepped out of line again, there happened to be one more piece of TNT waiting for them.

Greg and Megan got engaged. Life was good again. Brock was asked to be the Best man and he was thrilled to oblige. The couple planned a wedding by Lake of the Ozark's later that summer. Half of the town was invited. Troy Laurie call Del Phillips and secured the photographer. The River Piper offered catering at no charge. Nothing would be left out, except everyone's friend Buzz Wheeler.

The End

CPSIA information can be obtained
at www.ICGtesting.com
Printed in the USA
BVHW041538270821
615174BV00009B/153

9 780228 860051